Fools Gold

Lynn Lovegreen

Copyright 2013 Lynn Lovegreen
Cover Art by Joan Alley
Editing by Jacqueline Hopper

This book is a work of fiction and any resemblance to persons, living or dead, or places, events or locales is purely coincidental. The characters are the product of the author's imagination and used fictitiously.

Warning: The unauthorized reproduction or distribution of this copyrighted work is illegal. No part of this book may be scanned, uploaded or distributed via the Internet or any other means without the permission of Prism Book Group. Please purchase only authorized editions and do not participate in the electronic piracy of copyrighted material. Thank you for respecting the hard work of this author.

Published by Prism Book Group
ISBN- 978-1-940099-26-2
Published in the United States of America
Contact info: contact@prismbookgroup.com
http://www.prismbookgroup.com

DEDICATION

This is dedicated to my mother and father, who first taught me the power of words.

CHAPTER ONE

Southeastern Alaska, 1898

Ellie stood on the foredeck and watched the lush green coast pass by as the steamship chugged along. The fresh, cool breeze filled her lungs. A pod of killer whales broke the surface of the water in the distance, black and white bodies rolling, tall fins arcing toward the sky, then back into the ocean. The whales exhaled in puffs of spray. A seal rested on a small iceberg nearby, and Ellie couldn't help but smile as she surveyed its dark, liquid eyes, gray fur, and white whiskers.

A killer whale knocked the seal off the berg and seized it in its mouth. Ellie gasped as the seal struggled for life. When the killer whale rolled under the waves—seal still in its jaws—Ellie, pulse beating at her temples, leaned forward over the rail, staring at the spot where the whale descended.

"Careful, there." Ellie's breath halted as a pair of strong hands grasped her waist and lifted her up and away from the rail. Her bottom brushed against someone as she was set down on the deck.

"What do you think you're doing?" Turning to a wall of wool-clad chest, she looked up to see a young face with a thick, brown goatee and an arrogant smile.

"Pardon me, miss." A twinkle pierced the man's blue eyes. "If the ship had made a sudden move, you'd have been thrown into the water."

"Well, I never." Ellie dismissed him with a sniff. "I wasn't that far over the edge." She was not used to being manhandled and wouldn't put up with male condescension.

"My apologies, miss." The stranger tipped his hat. "May I introduce myself properly?" He extended his hand. "Duke Masterson at your service, headed for Skagway."

Giving his hand the minimum two shakes to be polite, she then started to turn away as Billy ran up to them, forcing an introduction. "Miss Ellie Webster, and this is my brother, Billy."

Billy and Duke shook hands heartily.

"Glad to meet you, Billy. Call me Duke. Are you headed to Skagway too?"

"Yep." Billy grinned. "First Skagway, and then the gold country."

"Ah, you're going to try mining?" Duke smiled.

"We're gonna get rich like everybody else," Billy declared.

Handsome Duke raised his eyebrows. "A lot of people already beat you there. But maybe you'll be lucky."

"My brother and I are not relying on luck." Ellie raised her chin. "We have determination and a good plan."

"I'm sure you do, Miss Webster." As he tipped his hat again, he was looking too closely at the cameo necklace on her bosom.

Another man with low thoughts on his mind, just like the farmhands back home. And he doubted they could strike it rich. She would not encourage him with any more of her attention.

Refusing to be familiar and use his first name, she said, "Goodbye, Mr. Masterson." She could still feel where he'd laid his hands on her waist.

Ellie turned on her heel, took Billy's arm, and walked away down the port deck.

"Why'd we have to leave so fast, sis?"

She didn't want to tell Billy about Duke's rudeness. It would only make him angry. "That is not the kind of person we should associate with," Ellie said, seeing the presumptuous man with his memorable blue eyes in her mind. "Just watch and let me do the talking when we meet people and, maybe one day, you'll pick up on these things on your own."

Her brother wasn't stupid, but had never used his brain much. That's why she was headed to the Klondike gold fields with him. Mama wouldn't let Billy travel on his own, fearing he was too easy a target for a thief or con man. But Billy was only seventeen to her eighteen, so maybe there was hope for him yet. In the meantime, with Billy's strength and Ellie's mind, they'd be able to make their fortune and save their family's farm.

Ellie looked up at Billy and patted his arm. "Come on, it's almost dinner time. Let's get back to our cabin."

DUKE'S PULSE DRUMMED a ragtime beat as Ellie and her brother walked away. Nice bottom beneath those skirts, didn't seem to be padded, and slim ankles inside those little boots. What a beautiful girl, Duke thought, though a bit snobbish. Clear complexion, brown eyes a man could swim in—definite assets to consider on a lonely night.

Judging from her sharp speech, Ellie didn't seem impressed with him. But she did have spirit, and that intrigued him. He hoped he'd run into her later. Of course, they were bound to meet again. The steamer was only so big, and it was still a few days before they reached Lynn Canal and Skagway.

Ellie Webster. He'd remember the name.

Dan Palmer tapped his shoulder. "Hey, Duke, what are you doing up here?"

"Nothing, partner, just enjoying the scenery."

Dan laughed as Duke watched Ellie and Billy for a moment. "Always noticing the ladies, aren't you?"

Ignoring his teasing, Duke asked, "Any news?"

"According to the captain, we should make it to town on Thursday. And Robbins says we can set up the saloon in Skagway, if we pay certain, ah, fees."

"We can handle that. Good to hear."

He'd chosen well when he'd brought Dan in on the business. His partner had already been helpful in getting the whiskey at rock-bottom prices. Duke figured it shouldn't be a problem to start the saloon, and then they'd make a bundle. No more working for someone else—they'd be the bosses. And they'd be living in style by this winter. This was going to be a summer to remember, all right.

Maybe the best in his twenty years.

"NOW MIND YOUR manners," Ellie admonished as she attacked Billy's mop of curly, brown hair with a brush. "Act like you're at the preacher's house." She moved to adjust his white, starched, linen collar so it wouldn't sit crooked on his gangly neck.

"I know, sis." Billy waved her hands away, then pulled his shirtsleeves down, trying to smooth the wrinkles out. "Not every day we're asked to have tea with the captain." He grinned.

Ellie smiled at her brother. He was so sweet when he was excited. She assessed her own clothing in the mirror. The white, lace collar showed above her blue traveling suit. The nicest clothes she had. Smoothing the jacket and A-line skirt as best as she could, she wished she had an iron. Who'd have guessed she'd mingle with top-notch folk out here on the ocean?

She stepped back to get the full effect in the mirror. Her figure had enough curves without using one of those unhealthy corsets to alter it. Mama had seen a picture of an emancipation bodice and made one for herself and one for Ellie. The white vest fit securely over her chemise and gave her figure support without those constricting stays some girls wore. Mama never had reason to be uncomfortable for fashion's sake, and Ellie saw her point. Of course, Ellie saw her point on just about everything.

Adjusting her cameo necklace for the hundredth time that day, she ensured it hung perfectly centered on her white blouse, and fingered it gently. The necklace was a present Papa and Mama had given to her the Christmas before Papa died. But she couldn't dwell on that now.

Ellie tucked a strand of wavy-brown hair under her hat, a blue one that matched her suit. The white veil was firmly fastened out of the way along the wide brim. She hoped the effect was neat but elegant.

"This is the first time we've socialized with real high-class people," Billy said.

"Yes, we want to make a good impression. I wish we'd brought an iron."

"Mama always says it's not the clothes that are important, but the person in them. They won't care about a few wrinkles."

"Let's hope so," she answered, but her tension lowered at the thought. Billy could talk sense now and then.

The ship changed course, making them both sway to the left for a moment. Taking a deep breath, she put her arm on Billy's.

"All right, shall we?" She gave him a brave smile and he escorted her down the passageway.

The captain's cabin was paneled in dark wood. The tables were covered in lace doilies, and photographs of scenery and portraits hung on the walls. Ellie admired the gleaming brass buttons on the captain's uniform and the pink roses painted on the dainty china tea service.

"Thank you for asking us to tea, Captain Barlow."

"I am grateful for your presence today." A grandfatherly man with gray hair and whiskers, the captain smiled and pulled out a chair for her. "Your feminine grace adds much to our company."

"Thank you." Ellie returned the smile, then wondered if he said that every time a woman was on board the ship.

The captain introduced them to the two gentlemen standing in the room.

"So, where are you from, Miss Webster?" asked the redheaded gentleman in the tan frock coat to her left, the one the captain had identified as Mr. Dan Palmer.

"Nebraska," Ellie answered, then nodded to Billy so he could elaborate.

"Our family lives on a farm in the middle of Nebraska, near the town of Red Cloud. We grow wheat, mostly, and a little corn, and raise cattle," Billy added.

"Smart to diversify nowadays." The captain poured and passed cups of tea to his guests. "Can't put all your eggs into one basket."

"True," said Mr. Jack Moore, sitting by the porthole. "We're in manufacturing back in Massachusetts, and it's better to have several products to sell, instead of one."

"My family's in agriculture, too." Mr. Palmer turned to Ellie. "I'm from central California, but I've been living in San Francisco lately."

"Beautiful city," Mr. Moore said.

"It is, well, most parts of it are." Mr. Palmer raised one eyebrow. "There are some places I wouldn't recommend to you, Miss Webster. But they have a fine opera house and other things you'd enjoy."

"I'm sure I would." Ellie smiled at him. Opera houses and San Francisco were of no particular interest to her, but he treated her like a lady. She decided she liked Mr. Palmer.

There was a pause as they all sipped their tea.

"Of course, you've visited Seattle, Miss Webster," the captain noted. "So you've been to a big city before. But San Francisco is more settled, has more culture."

Ellie thought of what little she'd seen of Seattle—the train station and the supply stores near the dock. The crowds of people had closed in on her as she'd walked down the boardwalks, but they'd been friendly enough when she and Billy had bought their provisions.

"And the weather in San Francisco is soft compared to Nebraska. Much milder," the captain said, then sipped his tea again.

"Not anything like the winters in the Klondike," Mr. Moore said as he added a lump of sugar to his cup.

"We'll be gone by winter—make our money and head home as soon as we can," Billy said, balancing his teacup and saucer on his knee in a way that made Ellie nervous. She debated whether she could discreetly tell him to move it to a safer place.

"You might," Mr. Palmer replied. "Some people have made money in a season, but mostly from hitting a lucky streak or mining the miners."

"What does 'mining the miners' mean?" she asked.

"Selling supplies to the miners or providing them services," the captain explained. "Or, in its worst meaning, conning them out of their money." He offered a plate of shortbread cookies. As delicately as Ellie could, she took one and ate it, trying to catch any crumbs in her lips before they could fall and make a mess on her skirt.

"Soapy Smith is the worst of that bunch. Stay away from him," the captain said.

"Who's Soapy Smith?" Billy asked.

Mr. Palmer took a cookie from the plate. "He's a con man, and he's in cahoots with most of Skagway's lawbreakers."

"Keep out of Jeff's Parlor, and don't send any telegrams," Captain Barlow added.

Mr. Palmer nodded. "There's no telegram service in Skagway—only people claiming there is one, to take your money."

Ellie put on a brave face. Skagway was starting to sound dangerous. "We'll steer clear of that," she assured them. "Is there mail service?"

"Yes, but not regularly. I can take a letter to mail for you when we depart Skagway, if you want to write home," the captain offered.

"Thank you. I'd like that." At least there were thoughtful gentlemen out here amongst the ruffians.

The cabin tilted to the right. Grabbing his saucer in time to save it from falling, Billy spilled tea on his wrist. Ellie patted it with her napkin as Billy's face turned crimson.

"It takes a while to get used to the movement on a ship," the captain reassured him.

"Good catch." Mr. Palmer had a twinkle in his eye. "Quick reaction time there."

Billy grinned, and Ellie was thankful for his kind attention to her brother.

"May I ask what your plans are, Miss Webster, after we dock?" the captain inquired.

"We're going to head up to the gold fields."

"I've seen a lot of people go up there, and quite a few come back to Seattle," Captain Barlow said. "So I hope you won't be offended if I offer more advice."

"Not at all. Please do."

He cleared his throat as he looked at Ellie. "Miss Webster, the gold fields and the way there is a long, rough journey. Your enthusiasm is admirable, but you're an elegant young woman and I'm not sure you know what it'll be like out there."

"Thank you, Captain. I know it will be difficult." Ellie straightened in her chair as her heart leapt at being called elegant. "My brother and I have our own reasons for going to the gold fields and we'll not be dissuaded. We'll be strong, when the time calls for it."

"I hate to see a nice, proper girl like you get out there and…" His voice trailed off, as if he realized it wasn't any use trying to talk her out of it. "The Chilkoot Trail is the fastest way to the Yukon River and the gold strikes. The alternate route is the White Pass Trail. They say pack animals can use it, but not easily. It's also known as Dead Horse Trail. No young lady would want to see how some of those men treat their horses. No need to put you through that when it's no advantage compared to the Chilkoot. The Chilkoot

Trail is the way you should take. You have the supplies the Mounties require?"

"Yes." Ellie thought of their gear in the hold of the ship.

"So you'll need to make several trips over many days, up the mountain, to get it all through the pass. Then you'll have to make a boat to cross Lake Bennett and the river beyond it. Have you built a boat before?" he asked Billy.

"No, sir." There wasn't any call for boats on the farm.

"Find an experienced partner to help you with that or pay someone to do it. You don't want to lose all your things in the lake."

Ellie kept her face still, but her stomach fluttered. "Thank you for your advice, Captain." Taking another cookie, she wondered how much money they'd need for the boat. The newspaper articles hadn't mentioned that.

Mr. Moore turned to Billy. "If we go up at the same time, I'd be happy to help you out. I watched my uncle build a skiff once."

"Thank you for the kind offer," Ellie interjected. "Perhaps we'll meet at the lake, if we're there at the same time." She was doubtful he'd be of any help to them. Surely someone with more experience than watching a skiff being built might be found.

Mr. Moore nodded. "Of course."

Mr. Palmer took another cookie. "I'd offer, but we're staying in Skagway."

"What are your plans in Skagway?" Mr. Moore asked.

"My partner and I are 'mining the miners.'" He grinned at the phrase. "We're setting up a saloon, no offense meant, miss."

"None taken." His sensitivity was appreciated. She'd never set foot in a saloon, but had no objection to them. "Mama always says, 'Everything in moderation, and one drink never hurt anybody'."

"If I can help you and your brother in Skagway, miss, just let me know," Mr. Palmer added.

"Thank you, Mr. Palmer," Ellie said.

"Please, call me Dan."

"Thank you, Dan." She felt a smile spread across her face.

A steward opened the door. "Excuse me, Captain. We're coming into Stephens Passage."

"Thank you, Johnson. Pardon me, folks. Duty calls." He bowed to Ellie. "Pleased to meet you, Miss Webster."

"My pleasure, Captain." Ellie started to her feet and the men around her stood in response.

"May I walk you back to your cabin?" Dan Palmer asked, raising his arm to her.

She gave him her best smile. "Yes, thank you." Ellie rested her hand on the crook of his elbow and Billy followed behind them.

"Nice man, the captain," Dan commented as they walked to her room.

"He is," Ellie agreed, visualizing the journey to the gold fields, her stomach tightening as she wondered how steep the pass was.

"I think he gave you good advice today."

"Yes. I appreciate him recommending the Chilkoot."

"Miss Webster, I know you must be very strong, living on the farm and all, but gold mining is hard and dirty work. It seems easier to me to stay in town and get a job there."

"You don't know Mama," Billy said behind them.

"Even your mama might reconsider if she saw what was involved."

"No, we've come all this way for the gold. We need to earn enough for the mortgage on the farm." Ellie thought of Mama at home, relying on them.

Dan nodded sympathetically. "Ah, many people are having trouble with their farms lately."

"Papa got a mortgage to pay for new farm equipment, and then he died of consumption, so we got behind on the payments," Billy added.

Dan's earnest face turned to her. "I'm so sorry for your loss."

"Thank you. If we strike it rich, that'll get us more money than a regular job," Ellie elaborated.

"Perhaps, but earning money in town is a sure thing, not like trying to hit pay dirt. I hope you will consider all of this carefully, once you get to Skagway and see the situation. Will you think about it?"

"Yes, I will. Here's our"—she searched her memory for the proper word—"stateroom."

"A pleasure to meet you, Miss Webster." Dan's blue eyes locked on hers, then he bent over her hand.

"Call me Ellie." A thrill passed through her as he kissed her knuckles. Nobody had ever kissed her hand back on the farm.

"Hope to see you again, Ellie."

Billy closed the door behind them. "Boy, we got a lot of good information today."

"Yes, we did."

"This is going to be harder than I thought," he said as he took off his collar.

"Yes, but the rewards might be greater too." She pulled the hatpins from her hat and set them on the chest. "You still want to go to the gold fields?"

"Sure, if you do. That Dan, he seems real nice."

"Yes, he does," she agreed. If things were different, she knew she could get sweet on someone like Dan, unlike that Duke Masterson. Her heart skipped unexpectedly as Mr. Masterson's impudent grin came to mind. Shaking her head at the thought, she reminded herself there were more important things to do here than waste time thinking about him. She had to keep Billy out of trouble and make money for the farm. If it meant climbing mountains and building boats, then she and Billy would do that. Whatever it took, she was up to it. There was no time for men, no matter how nice their manners were. Or weren't.

CHAPTER TWO

Ellie gazed at the hills passing by as the steamer made its way up Lynn Canal. Dark, green cedar and hemlock trees towered over dense emerald thickets next to the shining ocean. It was primeval forest—like the one mentioned in the Longfellow poem—not at all like the sweeping plains of her home. A coal-black raven cawed from a nearby tree, then glided above the water.

"Good morning, Miss Webster," a voice said in her right ear. She jumped and turned in time to see Duke Masterson tip his hat.

"Morning," she said, then turned back to the forest, irritated by his interruption.

"Lovely, isn't it?" The smile in his voice hung in the air for a moment as she enjoyed the view. A waterfall cascaded into the sea as the ship chugged along the inlet.

"Yes, it is," she said, her annoyance softened by the sight before her.

"I think it's the most beautiful place I've ever seen," Duke added as the waterfall faded into the distance.

At least he can appreciate fine scenery, Ellie thought as she smiled at him. His high cheekbones and long eyelashes framed his clear, blue eyes.

Duke caught her looking at him, and her cheeks turned hot. He grinned at her. "Yes, definitely the most beautiful place I've seen."

Ellie opened her mouth to speak, but couldn't think of anything to say. In her embarrassment, her face burned hotter. She was usually the one with a witty retort or comment to shut down impertinent people.

Whether to ease her feelings or for some reason of his own, Duke did not press his advantage further. He tipped his hat again, said, "Be seeing you, Miss Webster," and strolled down the deck and around the corner, out of sight.

Ellie noted his broad shoulders as he walked away. Don't make such a fuss, she told herself. *You've seen good-looking men before. Why should this one get you so discombobulated?* Her cheeks were still burning as she answered her own question. *I guess it's the combination of good looks and confidence. At any rate, I've got to stop mooning over him like a schoolgirl.*

Ellie observed a bald eagle perched in a cedar tree, its white head shining in the sun. It watched her, too, with its steely gaze. She wondered what it thought of the ship coming through its territory.

"Hey, little lady." A rough-looking man approached unsteadily from the bow of the ship, wearing dungarees and a torn jacket. "Enjoying the view?"

In response, she turned away from him.

"Anything I can do for you?" he hissed in her ear. Alcohol lingered on his breath.

"I beg your pardon," she answered. "Didn't your mother teach you any manners?"

He stepped back. "I'm sorry, ma'am. Thought you were one of those entertainers."

"Do I look like a saloon girl to you?" Ellie stood tall and looked down her nose at him.

"No, I apologize, ma'am." He slunk away, back toward the stern.

It occurred to Ellie she could get this kind of treatment often. The gold country might be more trouble than she expected.

"Who was that?" Billy asked as he joined her from the bow.

Ellie sniffed. "Some drunk."

"Oh, I'm sorry. I should have gotten rid of him for you."

Ellie's heart glowed at her little brother's attempt at chivalry. Maybe he'd be able to assist her as much as she could look out for him on this journey. But she didn't want him to think she needed help with every little thing that came along.

"Thank you, but I took care of it."

"Oh. I was talking to the crew. Got to see how the steam boiler works."

"I'm sure it was interesting."

"They can burn coal or wood, whatever is handy. Oh, look, there's an eagle."

"Yes, a bald eagle." It soared over the ship toward an island on the other side.

Billy's brown eyes were wide. "This sure is different from back home."

"Yes, it certainly is." Home seemed boring compared to Alaska.

"SKAGWAY!" THE STEWARD shouted as Ellie and Billy rushed to the deck with the other passengers. There it was, a few rows of wood buildings and white tents shining in the evening sunshine, nestled in a valley between steep, craggy peaks. Though it was late May, snow still coated some of them. Imagining a climb up those mountains with a load of supplies on her back, Ellie felt her heart beat faster. She focused on the lonely wharf sticking out into the inlet.

Dan Palmer appeared at her elbow. "It's late, Ellie. Better stay in town until you can get a boat to Dyea in the morning. My partner and I have a friend who can recommend a place."

Duke Masterson tipped his hat behind Dan. "Miss Webster, Billy."

Ellie's eyes widened. She'd expected someone more genteel to be Dan's partner. That explained why only Dan was invited to the captain's cabin for tea. The captain obviously didn't consider Duke a gentleman. But she had to admit, Duke looked handsome today, with his hair brushed neatly, and wearing his dapper, embroidered waistcoat and open sack coat, grinning at her as if he could hear her thoughts. Her face felt hot. She seemed to blush more around him than she did in a year.

"May we help with your supplies?" Dan asked.

"Yes, thank you."

After a little time and confusion, their tent, sacks and crates of food, and mining gear were gathered, and a wagon master was taking all four of them to Dan and Duke's friend in town. Ellie and Billy sat together on the seat, Dan and Duke behind them on top of the supplies. She turned and watched the wharf shrink, and then stole a glance at Duke. Ellie could tell that Billy and Duke were almost the same height, but Duke's broad shoulders and chest dwarfed Billy's thin frame.

Duke's family must be heavier than ours, Ellie thought as she tried not to stare at his masculine build. Dan was small in comparison—a short, stocky man who flashed his broad smile when he noticed her looking at him and his business partner.

Ellie held her hat to keep it more securely on her head as she viewed the scene around her.

"That's how the town got its name, miss," the wagon driver shouted over the din. "It means place of big wind."

Brisk gusts were blowing through the valley. The street was six inches deep in mud. A row of buildings lined each side, adorned with signs advertising the Pillbox Drug Company, the Burkhard House, Yukon Outfitters, and Getz and Donavon Packers. Wagons and horses were slowly winding their way past men walking by, as the boardwalks next to the buildings were full. People were milling around everywhere, in crowds that compared to those she'd seen in Seattle. Horses whinnied and the murmur of conversation added a hum to the air.

Men and boys shouted.

"Get the latest news on the gold fields!"

"Supplies, get your supplies at Henry's General Store!"

A mass of men in a variety of clothing—from bowler hats and dress pants, to hunting gear, to three-piece suits—walked next to them in the street or on the board sidewalks. Ellie glimpsed a woman's hat in the crowd, but lost sight of it as the lady disappeared through a doorway. She was the first woman she'd seen since Seattle—at least there were a few others out here.

Beyond the streets were tall hemlock and cedar trees skirting the green mountains, and snow patches were scattered along the slopes.

"Packers! Get your gear to White Pass! Packers!"

"Telegraph office on Broadway! Send your telegram home!"

Ellie and Billy exchanged knowing glances at the announcement. At least they knew to avoid that place, but she wondered if Billy would have gone in there if he'd been on his own.

It was still daylight, although it was almost ten o'clock in the evening, and the town didn't show signs of settling down for bed anytime soon. Back in Red Cloud, everyone would be asleep by now.

The wagon stopped in front of the Alaska Saloon and Hotel. Ellie misjudged her footing as she stepped off the wagon, and Duke caught her around the hips when she staggered. She was relieved that she didn't fall in the mud, but it did seem that Duke touched her every time he had the opportunity. As she glared at him, he released her and stepped back a pace.

They walked into the bar, Ellie's hand on Billy's arm, Duke and Dan behind them. Every set of eyes turned to them, and then focused on Ellie. She dug her fingers into Billy's coat and attempted to keep her expression impassive.

The saloon appeared as she had imagined it would, with a long, wood counter, a mirror behind it with shelves full of bottles, and small tables where men drank or played cards. The room was crowded, and the air smelled of whiskey and cigar smoke, and she wondered if all saloons were like this, like the ones she'd read about in dime novels.

"We're looking for Johnny Cartland," Dan told the man at the bar.

"Sure. Johnny!" he called into the back.

A red-faced man in an apron entered and scanned the crowd before seeing them. "Hey, Dan! Duke! You made it!" They shook hands heartily.

"These two are going to Dyea in the morning and they need a decent place to stay," Duke explained as he gestured to them.

"Oh, of course. Let me introduce you to my wife." Johnny indicated the entrance he'd just emerged from.

Duke chuckled. "You have a wife?"

"Love catches up with most of us."

Ellie wondered if Duke would ever fall in love. It seemed unlikely.

They walked through the saloon to a homey kitchen. A woman, heavy with child, with black hair and dark skin, closed the door of the wood stove before she stood, a hand on her lower back as she straightened.

"Here are some folks who need a place to stay tonight."

Rose took Ellie's hands in hers. "Welcome. We need more good women here."

Soon, the men were out front swapping stories with Johnny while Ellie and Billy were comfortably settled in the kitchen with Rose.

"Want another piece of pie, Billy?"

"No, thank you, ma'am. Three is my limit, I think."

Rose winked at Ellie. "Growing boy."

Billy pointed his fork at Ellie. "My sister bakes good pie, too."

"You could make money in Skagway, selling pie."

Ellie thought of the box oven among their supplies. "That's true, but we need to strike it big in the gold fields."

"Your choice, but baking's a lot easier than mining."

Ellie shook her head. "So how did you come to Skagway?"

"My father was one of the first settlers and my mother is a Chilkoot Indian. We've been here longer than most folks. Any questions you want to ask?"

"We're going to take the Chilkoot Pass to the gold fields," Ellie explained. "We know about the trail and Lake Bennett." As she thought of their conversation with the ship captain, her stomach fluttered.

"And you still want to go? You're a strong one." Rose stopped to take a bite of apple pie. "At least you're going in summer. Muddy, but not much snow. Big avalanche last month. Lots of people lost." She shook her head while pouring more coffee into their mugs.

"That must have been awful," Billy said.

Ellie sipped her coffee. "Once we get past the lake and all, what's it like out in the gold fields?"

"From what I hear, it's pretty wild country and a hard trail. But there is gold left to mine. You'll have to go out to the Grand Forks area or further north to find it. Once you get up there, you'll find sourdoughs who can tell you more."

Billy asked, "What are sourdoughs?"

"Oh, people who have been up here for a long time. Have to stay for a winter to be one."

Billy grinned. "I hope we get a lot of gold before winter."

"I hope you do." Rose smiled at him. "Talk to an old sourdough about how to pan for gold and what to look for. Don't want to waste your time with fools gold. That's the shiny stuff they call pyrite. Here, this is what real gold nuggets look like." Rose took a small jar from a shelf and poured a sprinkle of gold nuggets into Ellie's hand—gold-colored but dull, not bright like Mama's gold ring. Ellie showed them to Billy, then poured them back into the jar.

"Tonight, you will stay in our parlor upstairs." She waved away objections as Ellie opened her mouth. "Save your money for the trail, you never know when you might need something up there. I'll give you a good breakfast and you can get to the boat dock early to get someone to take you to Dyea."

"Thank you so much." The generosity of the people up north impressed Ellie.

"And when you get back to town to cash in your gold, you come see us. Okay?"

"We will."

"Should have a baby to show you, come fall." She patted her round stomach.

"Yes, we'll come visit your baby," Ellie promised.

THE SUN WAS already high in the sky as they finished breakfast in the kitchen the following morning. Ellie was helping Rose with the dishes when Duke Masterson appeared in the doorway.

"Morning, Miss Webster." He tipped his hat, grinning.

"Mr. Masterson," Ellie replied.

"Please, call me Duke. Thought we'd see you off."

Dan Palmer arrived with a mug of coffee in his hand. "Morning, everybody."

"Hey, Dan." Billy stood. "Should we get our stuff?"

"Let us help you with that."

Duke, Dan, and Billy loaded most of the supplies on a hired wagon. Ellie threw on a couple sacks of beans and flour to help out. Might as well start now, since she'd need to do her share of the work on the journey.

"This reminds me of the time my little brother wanted to run away." Duke easily set a crate of condensed milk into the wagon. "He was tired of everybody ordering him around, and announced that he was going to run away and become a cowboy. Must have been six or seven years old at the time." Duke set a sack on top of the crate. "I told him that he was going to need water in the desert, and he went in the house and came out with a canteen. Then I told him that he was going to need some food, too. Got a mug of dried beans, like this stuff here." He patted the sack on the wagon.

Ellie smiled as she realized where this was going and added a box to the wagonload.

"I told him he needed a bedroll and he got a blanket off his bed. So pretty soon he had a plate and utensils, a hat and coat." Duke's eyes twinkled as he put the tent on the wagon. "When I told him he might as well bring his pillow, he threw the whole lot down on the ground and hollered, 'Never mind, it's easier to stay here!'"

They all laughed as Billy placed the last crate on the wagon. The thought of Duke being a good big brother was touching.

Duke helped Ellie up onto the seat. His gaze met hers for a moment. Genuine concern showed in his piercing blue eyes as he spoke softly.

"Are you sure you want to do this, Miss Ellie?"

"Yes, I do."

"It's a hard road up ahead. I wish you the best of luck." His handshake was gentle.

"Thank you. We'll be fine." Ellie tried to swallow away the lump in her throat. She didn't know why seeing the caring side of Duke jumbled up her emotions.

Letting go of her hand, he said, "If there's anything I can do for you, I'll be happy to."

"*We'll* be happy to," Dan added.

"Thanks," Billy said as he sat next to Ellie.

"Good luck with your saloon," Ellie called as the driver urged the horses forward. Mud stuck to the wheels, making them start with a lurch.

Dan waved. "Good luck to you."

"Take care." Duke's eyes were locked on her. They followed her until the crowd came between them. Ellie faced forward, toward

Dyea and the trail ahead, hoping to meet Duke and Dan again one day, not sure which one she wanted to see most. Maybe there was more to Duke than she first thought.

DUKE WATCHED ELLIE and Billy disappear into the crowd, then stood there a moment longer, his chest tight as he considered what Ellie would have to face on the trail. Her iron will would probably be enough to keep them going, but he wished she wasn't so stubborn and had taken Dan's advice to stay in town. Ellie and Billy might have the strength, but did they have the luck to strike it rich?

Dan patted him on the shoulder. "If anybody can do well out there, it'll be those two."

"I guess you're right." He turned to his friend and headed back into the saloon with him. But Ellie's face kept playing in his mind. He hoped she'd be all right.

AS THE BOAT glided through the water, Ellie remembered saying goodbye to Mama a few weeks ago. Her wrinkled face had almost scowled as she'd emphasized the importance of their mission. Shaking her bony finger at Ellie, she said one last time, "You take good care of Billy, keep him safe and out of trouble. Make enough money for us to stay on the farm. And remember you're a lady."

"I will, Mama. I promise."

"Billy, you listen to your big sister and help her any way you can."

"Yes, ma'am."

"With your brothers Robert and Donald gone East and Papa passed on, you're the only ones left for me to depend on."

"I know, Mama. We'll make good money and come back as soon as we can," Ellie had promised.

"I'll hire the Miller boys to get me through harvest and the cattle sale. You just take care of yourselves."

"We will, Mama." Billy hugged her for the last time. Then Mama had held him at arm's length for a moment and studied his face. Ellie realized how hard it was for Mama to send her youngest boy off the farm, and it would be up to Ellie to bring him back safely. She was determined to do that, along with digging as much gold as they could in the Klondike.

The boatman rowed past the two land points west of Skagway and headed toward Dyea, a smaller town at the mouth of the Taiya River. Through the drizzling mist, Ellie could see the now-familiar white wall tents scattered along the winding river, interrupted by wood buildings here and there.

"Where's the trail?" Billy asked the boatman.

The scruffy man stuck his chin toward the river without pausing as he rowed the skiff to the beach. "Start walking past the town, you'll find the line of people soon enough."

He was right. Once they left the boat, Ellie and Billy walked through the mud in the same direction others were headed. They passed the buildings and found the line leading into the thick of the straight, tall trees that were like green giants guarding the path.

Ellie rushed to get a spot in line behind a gentleman in a bowler hat and three-piece suit, pack on his back. "Good morning, sir."

He started and turned. "Well, good morning, miss," he said with a British accent.

"Please, sir, can you save us this spot while we bring our things over?" She smiled as sweetly as she could and dumped her crate on the ground behind him.

"Oh, of course, I'd be delighted."

Billy and Ellie lugged their supplies, walking back and forth from the dock to the line.

"I'm Elliot Smith," Mr. Bowler Hat introduced himself after the second load.

"Ellie Webster."

"This is my son, Bert." He indicated the young man who unloaded a box of something at his feet.

"Good to meet you. Excuse me," she said as she left to get another load. As if there were no interruption in their conversation, she dropped a 50-pound sack of beans with their other gear and they continued.

It took fifteen trips to move the required one thousand pounds of staples. Ellie was glad she'd put on her work pants. They came in handy doing chores like threshing back home—much easier than dragging muddy skirts through the muck on the trail. The men were staring at her, maybe because of the trousers or because she seemed to be the only woman within sight. But that was their problem. She had work to do.

Ellie strapped her load to her back, as others did. Thank goodness they'd packed everything in sacks or crates so it wasn't too hard to carry, but her muscles started to feel the strain after a while. It was tedious work. As soon as they got it all in line with the other stampeders, they had to haul the supplies along the trail. All day, it was move a load, come back, move another load, and come back for another. At least mosquitoes weren't out in the drizzle.

"So where are you from, Miss Webster?" Mr. Smith inquired.

"Nebraska, where you are from?"

"England originally, lately from Chicago."

"Really? We have older brothers in Chicago." Billy dropped a crate on the ground. "Do you know Donald and Robert Webster?"

"Sadly no, but it's a very big town."

As she walked back to get another load, Ellie wondered what Mama was doing at that moment. Probably chores—feeding the horses, churning, mending, the usual routine—but Ellie hoped she was all right.

While Mama nursed Papa through his consumption last summer and fall, Ellie did most of the farm work with Billy. She was used to deciding what needed to be done in the fields, when to get the cattle to a new section for grazing. Now she was making different kinds of decisions and Mama was in charge of the farm. Ellie sighed as she thought of Mama all alone, waiting for them to strike it rich.

Another load to move, another snatch of conversation with Mr. Elliot Smith, and a big mud puddle to avoid. Then the drizzle stopped and a fresh, clean breeze rustled through the trees. Their tramp down the path went on for more than eight hours until they reached Finnegan's Point—a few tents next to the trail that served as rest stop for the night. Stampeders stopped to set up tents or sleep beneath the trees until morning. It was getting cooler, and she was glad they had wool blankets.

"Sis, you want me to set up the tent?"

Ellie looked at the haggard men, some rubbing their shoulders, some already asleep where they dropped, and couldn't imagine getting any trouble from this bunch. Privacy was a luxury on the trail.

"No, let's not bother tonight. Just dig out the blankets and mosquito netting." She arranged their supplies, putting the sacks of flour and dried beans on top, which would serve as their mattress. "Here, climb up and sleep next to me."

"Good night," Billy said, then yawned and fell asleep as soon as she draped the netting over them.

The next morning, Ellie and Billy found their blankets were damp. From then on, they'd have to assume it might rain during the night, and put up a shelter.

They ate the last of the biscuits and ham that Rose had given them, and started back in line. Ellie rubbed her shoulders and wondered if there was a better way to distribute the loads as they hauled the big bags and crates.

Trudging to the river, they paid the toll at the gate, and hiked across the bridge and up the muddy trail. Mud caked their boots, and there was a line of brown dirt across the bottom of her work pants.

Ellie and Billy hauled their supplies in front of young Bobby Joe from Louisiana, who missed home cooking and talked about food for most of the day.

"Have you ever had crawfish, Miss Ellie?" His Southern drawl elongated his words. "They're kind of like shrimp, but not really. You can boil them up or cook them with a gumbo—that's rice, and okra, and a mess of other things. Probably don't have that in Nebraska." Bobby Joe put down his load and stopped to scratch a mosquito bite under his shaggy, brown hair.

"No, but it sounds delicious," Ellie answered. The talk helped keep her mind off her sore back. She stepped carefully over a log across the trail then dropped the bag of beans to fetch the last load. "No gumbo back home, but my mama and I make good steak and potatoes, and pie."

Billy set down a crate. "Ellie makes the best apple pie in Nebraska."

"Wish you could make one of your apple pies for us here. Now, my mama can make the best pecan pie you ever tasted. Sweet, but not too sweet. It's the kind of syrup she uses. She buys it from a farmer who's up the river a ways." His brown eyes grew misty at the thought.

"I'm sure it's wonderful, Bobby Joe. How does she make her pie crust?" She ignored the curses of the man in front of them who had stepped in a puddle, and skirted the edge of another.

"The secret is cold butter, and she adds a little bit of flour at a time. It's the flakiest crust...." Bobby Joe sighed at the memory.

Ellie softened at Bobby Joe's sigh. He may have been scruffy in appearance, but Bobby Joe was a good man, missing his mother's cooking. She guessed you really couldn't tell a book by its cover, when it came to men.

Her brother broke in. "So, Bobby Joe, what's the hunting like down there in Louisiana?"

"Tons of things. Coons, and muskrats, and wildfowl." Bobby Joe stopped to swat at a mosquito. "What's up your way?"

"We got birds, too, grouse and passenger pigeons. There's big stuff too, like buffalo and antelope if you know where to look."

"Good eating, I bet." Bobby Joe's mind always returned to food.

They stopped at Canyon City and decided to pay the price to use the tramway through the next section of trail to gain time. Ellie, Billy, and Bobby Joe hiked through Dyea Canyon—sharing plenty of mud and cooking stories—and spent the night at Pleasant Camp. They were too tired to bother with the fire after dinner that evening, even though fires were supposed to keep the mosquitoes at bay.

The mosquito bites on her body were so thick, she stopped counting after a dozen. And her lower back was bothering her. She tried not to think about the Pass coming up,
but they kept up with the other men in line, and every hour took them further down the trail, closer to their goal.

"Cheer up, Billy," she told him when he lagged behind near the end of the day. "Just a few more weeks of this and we'll be in gold country. Think of all the money we're going to make up there."

"Yep," Billy answered with a gleam in his eyes. "Gonna hit paydirt. We'll have some left over after the mortgage, and we'll get Mama a new kitchen stove and a feather bed, too."

"You bet we will. But we have a little more of this traveling to do first." She scratched a mosquito bite on her neck.

Ellie inhaled and smelled the mud and sweat around her. The crowd was growing less scrupulous about their toilette. Most men had stopped bathing, stopped shaving, so unkempt beards were everywhere. Even Billy had a little stubble, and Ellie had limited herself to a quick splash of water to her face and hands each morning. Her hair was in a braid then pinned up to keep it out of the way.

Dappled sunshine played through the branches of the trees. Pink, wild roses bloomed nearby. The men alternated between optimism and sheer boredom.

"Getting close to where the streets are paved with gold!" someone shouted behind them.

"Don't believe everything you hear," another man grumbled. "Lots of guys get to the Klondike and go broke."

Ellie's heart fluttered as she wondered if she'd be one of the unlucky ones. But she wiped the thought from her mind and focused on picking up the next crate.

A tall man ahead of them groused, "Moving our loads day after day—seems like we'll never get there."

"Oh, the real work will come soon enough. Quit your b—" The grizzled man behind him noticed Ellie. "Excuse me, miss. Quit your complaining, mister. Hey, anybody know a good song?"

Someone started a chorus of *My Old Kentucky Home*, and Ellie smiled as she dropped her load and turned back for the next one. That song was popular back home, and she found herself thinking of Mama waiting for them. Just getting to the gold fields was hard, but what if they were wrong and couldn't strike it rich? They had to make their fortune somehow.

The next day they reached Sheep Camp, and the trees thinned out as they climbed in elevation. Ellie and Billy lost track of Bobby Joe as they traveled along with the crowd. There were fewer tree roots to step over. Her back was not as sore anymore, her body getting used to the loads. But she missed the company of women and the warmth of a wood stove on chilly nights. She envied Dan and Duke living comfortably in Skagway, but she was going to stick it out and get that gold for Mama.

The next stop was the Pass—the Scales, also called the Golden Stairs—the steepest part of the Chilkoot Trail. Ellie gulped as she looked up at the 35-degree slope and saw the line of stampeders struggling with their loads. A raven croaked as it flew over them, reminding her of Poe's poem, and she half expected it to say, "Nevermore."

"A lot of people turn around here," someone said behind her. "No one would think the less of you, miss."

As if to prove his point, a stampeder fell and started to tumble down the slope. One man stepped out of line to break his fall, then resumed his own climb.

"What do you think?" Ellie said to Billy. "We've made it this far."

Billy faced the line then met her eyes with a steely gaze. "Let's try it."

Ellie slapped him on the back. "All right, let's."

It was the most difficult thing Ellie had ever done, to keep her balance with a crate on her back and make her way up the slope. Her legs burned after the first couple of hours. It took six hours for one trip, and there were fifteen loads for Ellie and Billy—
split over ten days. No one made conversation on this part of the trail and, at first, Ellie kept her mind busy by reciting poems she'd learned in school, writing letters in her head to Mama, or wondering why the Canadian government thought they had to have so many pounds of beans in the first place.

Duke Masterson's face appeared in her mind once. The memory of his neat, dark goatee and clean-shaven cheeks looked mighty handsome next to the scraggly, bearded faces around her. But, after a while, her mind went blank and she focused on the task at hand.

The trail was a muddy cut in the slope, worn by thousands of human feet. Every time Ellie inhaled, a mix of male sweat, mud, tobacco, and wet wool filled her nostrils. Over the days they hauled their supplies up the mountain, her muscles were tired, but her back and legs grew stronger. She understood now what people meant when they talked of men grown into beasts. That's all she was now, a beast of burden, carrying loads of supplies, not even trying to think about anything except taking her next step.

At the summit, in the midst of the howling wind, the North-West Mounted Police collected customs at the Canadian boundary line and checked to make sure everyone had the required year's worth of food and supplies for each person—350 pounds of flour, 150 pounds of bacon, 100 pounds of beans, and so on.

Their money was safely stowed, Ellie wouldn't say where to the Mountie, but it was distributed in her bodice, right boot, and Billy's left boot. The uniformed Mountie was polite when he checked Ellie and Billy's belongings, tipped his broad-rimmed hat, and said, "Good luck, miss."

They'd made it through the Scales, but Lake Bennett and other unknown obstacles still lay ahead. Maybe the Mountie's words were meant to comfort her. Instead, they sent dread down her spine.

DUKE MASTERSON AND Dan Palmer were tending bar in their wall tent saloon that evening. The saloon was packed as always. It seemed as if every miner and townsman could spare fifty cents for a shot of whiskey. Men with mud from the trail on their clothes sat next to men in clean, pinstriped suits. Laughter and stories flowed as Duke wove his way between the rough-hewn tables and Dan poured drinks behind the bar.

They enjoyed having their own place. No one to answer to except each other, and Duke and Dan agreed on most things. Duke knew he could trust his partner. They'd been best friends ever since Dan had saved him from a knife fight in San Francisco. Now here they were, making good money, and at the end of the summer they'd have enough set aside to start their own saloon in San Francisco. That would be the good life.

He smiled at the thought of quality brandy, central heat, and a warm, feather bed. But somehow it didn't feel as he'd expected. Something was missing from his life, something needed to complete the picture.

"So that's when he said, 'What about the moose?'" A bald miner finished his story to a roar of laughter.

A customer jabbed his glass in Duke's direction, unsteady enough that the gesture took him off balance for a moment. "Another one, barkeep."

"Sorry, you've had enough, sir. Let me get you some coffee." Duke deftly traded the man's glass for a mug.

The customer stood, tottering, but sat down as Duke towered over him. "Well, all right."

"Hey, Duke, did I show you my nuggets?" A gentleman with a white, handlebar mustache held a constellation of gold nuggets in his hand.

"Nice. You found some big ones."

"Going to have them made into a bracelet for my wife."

"Great idea. She'll love it." Duke patted him on the back as he went to the next customer.

He wondered if Ellie and Billy were in gold country yet. They'd only met three times, just a couple weeks ago, but he thought about her often—those big brown eyes, pink cheeks, ample, curvy hips, and that strong will. She was prettier than most of the women in Skagway, even the entertainers, but, more than that, there was something about her that stood out—her strength of character. He hadn't met anyone like her before, and he wished he could help her somehow.

He crossed back to the bar to pick up a new bottle of whiskey. "Hey, Dan, have you heard any more about Ellie and Billy? Anyone see them?"

Dan laughed. "Gee, that came out of the blue. Are you sweet on her?" He waved his hand as Duke glared at him. "No, nothing since that guy passed them at the toll bridge. Why?"

Duke tried to sound casual. "No reason. Just wondering."

THE TRIP DOWN the other side of the mountain was muddy, but easier than the climb up. The slope became more gradual, and their neighbors started to talk to them again. There was still no sign of Bobby Joe and she wondered if he'd made it up the Golden Stairs.

The trail led down into the forest. Ellie turned her ankle on a rock, but tried to ignore the pain, and continued walking. At Lindeman, where the stampeders built boats for the twenty-mile trip across Lake Bennett, Billy declared that the worst of the trail was over.

To celebrate this point in the journey, Ellie and Billy decided to take a day off and camp there before getting a boat ready, moving their supplies to a spot next to a cluster of tents. Billy set up their wall tent while Ellie built a fire and started frying bacon.

A familiar laugh sounded behind her. "Hey, Miss Ellie, you made it! Good for you!"

"And you, too, Bobby Joe. Want some bacon?" she asked as she hugged him.

"I would *love* some." He plopped down next to her with a grin.

Ellie turned the bacon slices. "I can get some biscuits going in a minute."

"Ellie Webster, if you added some gumbo to that I'd marry you in a second."

Ellie laughed in reply. "No gumbo in the sacks. Sorry." It was a joke, but she took the marriage proposal as a compliment.

"Or in mine, I'm afraid. But I'll settle for a biscuit or two."

Billy gazed out at the lake. "Bobby Joe, do you know how to build a boat?"

"Certainly do. I been thinking we're gonna need one soon."

"You wanna build one together?"

"Sure. No sense in building a whole boat for only one man."

"You're the expert, and I'll do whatever work you tell me to," Billy offered.

"Guess you've proven you're strong enough." Bobby Joe nodded toward the trail behind them. "Okay, I'll tell you what to do."

Indicating her approval of his decision, Ellie smiled at Billy as she drew her shawl around her shoulders. She would have asked Bobby Joe if he hadn't. Her little brother was developing some common sense.

A FEW DAYS later, they christened their boat the *Ellie Marion*, and tested it on Lake Lindeman. It accepted the weight of the three people and their supplies. Ellie started breathing again when the boat showed no sign of leaks. Billy and Bobby Joe insisted on being chivalrous and doing all the rowing and, after a couple attempts, Ellie let them.

It felt almost sinful to be lazy after the last few weeks' work. Watching the green shore drift away as they moved along, she noted the patches of snow on the mountains, gazed at the bald eagles circling in the blue sky, and said, "Wonder what the poor people are doing today."

Billy laughed at their father's old saying. "Yep."

"Hard to find a more beautiful place," Bobby Joe agreed. "Here's Bennett coming up. We'll stop here and cross Lake Bennett tomorrow."

Finding a spot among the few rows of white tents and a crowd of tired men, they spent the night at Bennett. Bobby Joe and Billy talked to some veterans of the area to learn the best way to get across the lake and through the rapids.

As Ellie packed their gear more efficiently the next morning, she wondered what Mama was doing back in Nebraska, and what she'd think about their journey so far. This was the longest she had been away from home in all of her eighteen years. She missed talking to Mama, but consoled herself with the idea that she'd next see her mother when she presented her with the money needed to save the farm.

She hoped.

A flotilla of boats joined them as they prepared to cast off—skiffs, rowboats, and rafts with sails up to catch the wind blowing across the lake. Billy and Bobby Joe got the boat in the water and started rowing. The scene reminded Ellie of a barn raising, the way every one greeted them with high-spirited whoops and howdy-dos. She recognized a group of men from the trail, and turned to see them just as their boat sprang a leak and they headed back to the shore.

"Don't worry. They'll fix it," Bobby Joe assured her.

Soon, the crowd quieted as they concentrated on the work at hand. And the boats spread out, some cruising along while the slower ones fell back. The *Ellie Marion* pulled alongside the frontrunners. They were going to make it across the lake.

"Hang on, this is the tricky part," Bobby Joe called as the end of the lake narrowed and the sound of rushing water grew louder. The boats nearby either shot past them or lagged behind as they moved into a single-file line. Billy and Ellie leaned closer to Bobby Joe to hear him better.

"Okay, we've distributed the supplies as evenly as we can. If it starts to tip, grab the nearest valuable thing and get low in the boat. Hopefully, we won't lose anything important."

Ellie's eyes widened. Lose anything important? She made sure her cameo necklace was tucked under her blouse and glanced around to make sure the gear was secure. Then they were flying along the river, and Bobby Joe was shouting instructions to Billy about how to keep the boat pointed in the right direction. Ellie sat lower in the boat and held the tin box oven with her right arm while she grasped the gunwale with her left. Her heart pounded. *Dear Lord, please keep us safe. Let us reach the other side.*

The roaring grew louder and the trees passed by even more quickly as the rapids came into view. Bobby Joe shouted to Billy as they used their paddles to steer away from the boulders. Ellie's stomach lurched as they pitched to the right. Waves of frigid water hit her face, making Ellie gasp and blink.

Something slammed into the left side of the boat. They careened over a wave. Thoughts ran through her mind of Mama back home and the two promises she'd made—to keep Billy safe and strike it rich. They had to make it through this.

Ellie heard a crack as a rock hit the wooden hull. Water poured in. Bobby Joe shouted to hang on. He and Billy worked their paddles. Then the world became an icy, liquid place as she was pulled into the current. The cold shocked her body and she struggled to breathe. The water tossed her around like a leaf in a storm as she fought to keep her head above the surface. It struck her that she could die now.

That was her last thought before she lost feeling in her arms.

CHAPTER THREE

DUKE POURED A sarsaparilla for a Salvation Army Lieutenant. She was prettier than any lieutenant he'd seen before.

"Thank you, sir."

"No, thank you, Miss, er, Lieutenant, for gracing our presence. What should I call you?"

She chuckled. "Emma is fine."

It was nice to see a lady in town. Most of the women in Skagway were saloon girls or women for hire, and while he respected their right to make a living, he missed the honorable elements of society. Reminded him of the women back home in Red Cloud, and Ellie. He wondered where she was now.

"So, Emma, how is the mission?"

She shook her head. "Slow going. Many souls left to save. But we are making progress. Had a big group at our services this morning."

"Glad to hear. Keep up the good work."

She reached for her reticule. "How much do I owe you?"

"Nothing. It's on the house." He gave her a smile but his mind was still on Ellie. Something was missing from his life, and money wasn't it.

WHEN SHE AWOKE, Ellie was lying on a rock, the box oven under her arm. She sat up then inhaled sharply while the world spun. A quick glance around told her she was alone.

"Billy!" she yelled as loud as she could, the sound making her wince as her head pounded.

"Ellie?" Her heart skipped as she heard a familiar voice downriver. Billy was on a rock near the shore, blood covering his forehead. Her brother blinked and looked at her. "Bobby Joe there?"

Ellie scanned the area around them, but didn't see anyone. "Bobby Joe!" she shouted, then winced again.

No answer.

"Bobby Joe!"

She viewed the rocks at the edge of the rushing water, but couldn't see anything that resembled a person. Maybe he was downriver. She'd look for Bobby Joe later.

Ellie took an inventory of her own condition—cold, wet, and her head was throbbing. She checked her arms and legs. There didn't seem to be broken bones, but she was starting to shiver. She needed to get warm soon, and Billy probably did, too.

"I'll come over there," she called to her brother as she surveyed the safest route to his rock. Pieces of wood and bits of supplies were floating in the eddies and resting on rocks nearby. The water roared, but they were safe along the edge of the river.

"I'm coming," she said as she picked up the box oven and made her way over to his rock. Luckily, it was flat and big enough for two people. "Billy, are you okay?"

"I don't know." He let her push his wet hair aside and mop his forehead with her sleeve. A great deal of blood flowed from what seemed to be a shallow cut. She felt his arms, ribs, and legs, but didn't find any broken bones. He was shivering and had scratches and bruises, too.

Another boat came around the bend. She waved to the men on the boat, not sure if they saw her, they were so intent on getting their own boat through safely. One waved back and shouted something she didn't understand. At least someone knew they were here.

Ellie ripped off the sleeve of her blouse and bound up Billy's cut. "You think you can move?"

He nodded.

"Let's see if we can get to shore and warm up."

Leaning on each other, they scrambled from rock to rock until they reached the riverbank. Thank goodness she'd kept a few matches in her bodice. One was dry enough to light. They built a fire and huddled together, too exhausted to look for Bobby Joe. Ellie fell asleep wondering where he was.

A HORSE NICKERED. Ellie reached for her horse, Blaze. She petted his brown, velvety nose in the warmth of the barn.

"Miss," a voice said. She opened her eyes to see a man wearing a Mountie hat. "I'm Sergeant Jacobs. We're here to help you."

Ellie remembered the boat wreck. Billy's head was heavy on her shoulder, and she turned to see if the bleeding had stopped. Caked blood had dried on his bandage, but it was still oozing.

"He's going to be all right," the Mountie said as he gently lifted Billy off her shoulder. An older man looked at her brother closely while Billy blinked at him quietly.

"Do you know where you are?" the man asked.

"The rapids," Billy answered as he looked at Ellie. She nodded to him.

"I'm a doctor. Let me take a look at you." He checked Billy over. "What hurts the most?"

"My head," Billy answered. "And my hand."

Ellie wished she'd checked his hands. And where was Bobby Joe? "Sergeant, have you seen Bobby Joe?" she asked. "He was on the boat with us."

"I'll search for him now," the Mountie said as he started toward the river's edge.

Ellie glanced at the box oven next to her and couldn't help but smile. She'd grabbed the important stuff, like Bobby Joe had said to do.

The doctor asked Ellie, "Anything hurt?"

"My head. I think I hit it on a rock."

The doctor examined her, said, "Watch my finger," and waved his index finger back and forth in front of her face. She forgot to do that with Billy after the wreck. Mama did the same thing whenever a mule kicked someone in the head.

"Your Bobby Joe, he has long, dark hair?" the Mountie asked solemnly as he came through the brush toward her.

"Yes, he does."

"I'm sorry, miss. He's dead."

Why couldn't she cry? She'd cried buckets when Papa died last winter…why couldn't she cry now? She tried to stand up, but the world started spinning again.

"Have a seat, miss. You've had quite a shock."

Duke's face appeared before her eyes, smiling at her. Was he there? Where was Billy? "Billy?"

"I'm here, Ellie."

How were they going to get to the gold fields now? She stood, more slowly this time, to gather all their belongings together.

"Miss, just sit down there," the Mountie directed.

"Our things," Ellie explained.

"Sit down, please. We'll get them for you."

There was ringing in her ears and she felt dizzy. Why was she tired all of the sudden?

DAYLIGHT. WHITE LIGHT. Ellie opened her eyes and saw the tent wall. She remembered cold water, the boat. The rapids. But Billy was okay.

Gingerly she sat up, remembering the world spinning around last time. Except for the dull throb in her head and ringing in her ears, she felt much better.

"Hello there, you're awake." A plump woman with blonde hair smiled down at her, hands on her hips.

"Is Billy here?"

"Yes, he is. Billy, your sister's up," she called through the doorway of the tent. "I'm Mrs. Novak. Been looking after you for my husband, Doctor Novak. Glad you're feeling better."

Her brother entered the tent. He had stitches on his forehead, and his right hand was bandaged.

"Hey, sis. The doc said you got a big hit on the head. A concussion. But you'll be all right."

"You have stitches." She touched them gently. "And what happened to your hand?"

He held it up so she could see the two fingers wrapped together. "Broke the little finger. But it should heal okay. We just got banged up a little."

Mama told her to do two things, strike it rich and take care of Billy, and she'd failed at both. Ellie reached for the cameo on her chest, realized she was wearing a strange blouse and skirt, and looked around the tent for her belongings.

"Your clothes are washed and drying, and the rest are by your feet, money in a safe place." Mrs. Novak smiled. "Nothing to worry about. Want some tea or something to eat?"

"Tea, thank you."

The tin cup warmed her hands. She blew the hot steam onto her face before she sipped the strong, black tea, thinking of all their supplies and wondering if they could make it down the trail now. Tears came to her eyes when she remembered Bobby Joe.

"Well, well, our patient is awake." She recognized the speaker as the doctor who'd checked them over on the shore. His wrinkled face creased as he smiled. "I'm Doctor Novak. Watch my finger," he said as he moved it in front of her eyes. Then he felt her forehead. "Looking much better. Any pain?"

"A little headache and ringing in my ears."

"That'll fade in time. Your quick thinking probably saved your lives. I'm glad you started that fire so quickly. Did my wife and your brother catch you up on everything?"

"I guess so. Where are we, exactly?"

"Next stop after the rapids, Annie Lake."

"How long have we been here?"

"A couple days, counting today."

Ellie remembered fainting at the river, but that seemed as if it'd happened a minute ago. The Novaks must have done a great deal for her and Billy since then. "Thanks to both of you for all your help."

"You're very welcome." Mrs. Novak smiled. "Nice to see another woman out here."

"We'll let you talk to your brother for a bit. Too bad he's right-handed, but that finger should heal in six weeks or so," the doctor said as he and Mrs. Novak left the tent.

Guilt lodged itself like a lead weight in the bottom of her stomach. She hadn't kept Billy safe. "Does your finger hurt?"

Billy sat next to her on the cot. "Some. You feeling okay?"

"I guess so."

"Remember what happened to Bobby Joe?" he asked softly.

"Yes." Tears welled up in her eyes again and she tried to swallow away the lump in her throat. "You know, he almost proposed to me. It was kind of a joke, but…" She wiped her wet cheeks with the sleeve of the borrowed blouse.

Her brother put his arm around her shoulders. "He was a great guy. We buried him in a pretty spot near the river."

It was hard to believe she'd never see Bobby Joe again, and so unfair. They sat silently for a moment as she sniffed. What were they going to do now?

"Did they find our supplies?"

"We have twenty-three dollars, the box oven, the tent, some rope, a blanket, some bacon, the frying pan…"

Her heart thudded as she said, "Not enough to go on."

"No, you're right."

"Guess we'll have to go back."

"Yep. But maybe we can try the pie business in Skagway."

"It's not the same," she said. How would they be able to save the farm with a few apple pies?

Hot tears streamed down her cheeks and she turned toward Billy. He held her against his chest and let her cry. Bobby Joe was dead, their dreams of gold gone. She'd failed, even though she'd prayed and tried so hard. All that work, all the hours of climbing up to the Scales, and now they were finished, left with nothing. And Billy had a broken finger. What if it didn't heal properly?

She sobbed out her frustration, her grief, her anger at God for taking Bobby Joe away and letting this happen. Chest heaving, she cried until the tears were spent. Then she took a shuddering breath as she sat up.

"I'd give you a handkerchief, but I lost it," Billy said.

Lost it.

That wasn't all they'd lost.

"I guess all we really have is each other, and you never know when you're going to lose someone you care about."

"No, you don't." Billy squeezed her hand with his left one.

MRS. NOVAK INSISTED that Ellie and Billy spend another night with them before they headed back to Skagway. "You need rest, and I haven't had a chance to have any women's talk with you."

"Oh, all right, but let me help with the cooking."

"So, Billy, let's make pegs for that tent of yours," Dr. Novak offered.

"Okay. Ellie, can you mend the canvas on the tent?" Billy asked before the men started into the woods.

"Sure, right after we get supper going."

Ellie grabbed a bucket and went for water to soak the beans. Heart pounding at the sound of the rushing river, she took a deep breath and completed the task. *I can't avoid water just because of* the accident, she told herself, wanting to help with the chores and be less of a burden on the Novaks.

Ellie set the bucket by the stove. "Mrs. Novak, please use some of our bacon tonight."

"No, you'll need that later."

"This is our contribution for supper tonight, as a thank you for all your help." She put the wrapped bacon in Mrs. Novak's hand.

"We came up here to help people. It's our calling," Mrs. Novak said with a shake of her head.

"Please, let us thank you in this small way."

Mrs. Novak looked at the bacon for a moment. "Well, perhaps a little, to add flavor." She set the bacon aside and poured water into the bowl of beans to soak. "Did I tell you, we have a niece about your age back home?"

"No, you didn't." She unrolled the canvas and found a couple jagged tears near the entrance flap.

"Let me get some needles and thread." Mrs. Novak rummaged in a box. "My niece, Ermaline, is a great quilter. She did a crazy quilt for her hope chest. It has eight different kinds of stitches on it."

"My, she is good. I'm afraid I'm not that handy." Ellie laid the canvas between them so they could both work on a different tear. "My mending is all right, but I'm not an embroidery artist." She took the needle and thread that Mrs. Novak offered her. The bright white thread would stand out on the dingy material, but it would repair the tears in the canvas. "I'm a good cook, though."

Mrs. Novak smiled at Ellie. "Billy told me."

Trying to force away the urge to cry by sheer will, she sighed and looked down at her section of the canvas for a moment. "Guess we'll have to make pies in Skagway for a while."

"It's good you're both well enough to walk back to do that."

"Yes." Ellie touched the tingling spot on her temple, right above the hairline. At least she and Billy were mostly all right. But poor Bobby Joe. And who knew how many others had died there.

Mrs. Novak echoed her thoughts. "Your boat isn't the first to wreck on those rocks. Maybe it was Providence that kept you safe and stopped you from going further up the trail. You'll make a lot of money selling pies in town, maybe more than you could have up in the gold fields. It's a very good plan."

"Thank you." Ellie tried to focus on making her stitches even, swallowing around the lump in her throat. She was afraid she'd cry if she looked at Mrs. Novak. Maybe she was right. The Lord was supposed to work in mysterious ways. But it didn't seem right that Bobby Joe died.

Mrs. Novak snipped the thread from her canvas. "There we are. I'll get the fire going while you finish mending."

THE NEXT MORNING, after sharing goodbye hugs, Ellie and Billy were alone on the trail again. Ellie tried not to stare at Billy's right hand, but the sight of his bandage still left a pang in her gut.

The supplies that they'd managed to salvage were tied up into two, small packs. Instead of all the loads they'd carried up the trail, Ellie and Billy only had one a piece. They walked slowly this time, letting their bumps and bruises heal. Ellie's heart sank as they trudged through the trees, and she barely noticed where they were on the path.

No more dreams about striking it rich on the gold fields. No more Bobby Joe.

Tears welled up in her eyes as she remembered how Bobby Joe used to go on about pecan pie and crayfish. She didn't even know his last name or hometown, so they couldn't notify his family of his death. Maybe she'd made the wrong decision to push on at the Scales or to encourage Billy and Bobby Joe to build the boat. Had they been too greedy and losing everything, Bobby Joe included, was their punishment? She wished she could talk to Mama about it. Mama always viewed things thoughtfully and knew what to do.

"Maybe we should have turned around at the Scales," Ellie told Billy when they stopped for the night.

"Sis, we had no way of knowing what was going to happen." Billy slapped a mosquito on his left arm then winced. "You can't use hindsight here."

"Your hand hurt?"

"Some."

It must have been a significant pain for her brother to admit it so easily. Blinking away tears, Ellie rubbed her sore ankle. Because of her, Billy was injured and Bobby Joe was dead.

"Thinking of Bobby Joe?"

She nodded.

Mama's decisive tone rang in Billy's voice when he said, "He knew the risks, same as us. I'm sorry he's gone, but it's not your fault."

"I guess so, but it's really not fair."

"No, it's not fair. But there's nothing you could have done."

"You know, you're right, Billy." She took a deep breath, stood, and untied her pack. "I've got to quit fussing about it. Let's set up for the night." She'd have to think about it later. Right now, she had to get Billy to Skagway without further injury and see if they could make money baking pies.

A FEW MINERS were walking the trail from Bennett, taking the less risky, but much slower way around the lake. Men walked by with dusty clothes and wild-looking eyes, nodding at them silently, or staring down at their feet as they passed. The season was getting on and the stampeders needed to get to the gold fields quickly if they had any hope of making a go of it before the frost hit.

None of the men would know that she'd given up on striking pay dirt. They'd assume Ellie and Billy were going to Skagway to cash in their gold or to get more supplies. But she knew they were heading back for good.

Scanning the sloping green and white mountains around them, she found herself thinking, I'll never see this place again. On the other hand, she was relieved they wouldn't have to double back for supplies, especially at the Scales. One trip down that steep grade would be more than enough.

The mud had dried into dust on the trail. On windy days, they tried not to kick it up into the air where it formed silty, choking clouds. Ellie remained silent, thinking about their predicament, or wondering what Mama was doing back home. When she felt like talking, Ellie and Billy discussed their plans about what to do when they arrived in Skagway. The first stop would be at Johnny and Rose's place, to say hello and ask them where they could pitch their tent. Then they'd need to find out if they had to get a license or permission to set up a business in town, buy supplies and the ingredients for pies, and start their new pie stand.

"Hey sis, maybe we can say howdy to Dan and Duke, too." Billy absentmindedly rubbed his hand and she knew it was bothering him.

"Yes, we should." Ellie pictured the twinkle in Duke's eyes when he'd told them the story of his runaway brother, then his concern as they left for the trail. Duke was a kind man, even if he was a little cocky.

"Hope they're doing well with their saloon."

"Oh, they should be." Ellie didn't know much about business, but she couldn't imagine a bar not making money in a gold rush town like Skagway. "Is this a good place to stop, do you think?"

"Sure, fine with me."

They unloaded their packs in a clearing in the trees. The box oven clattered to the ground as Ellie untied her pack to get the tent. The oven had survived the wreck, with only one dent that Billy managed to tap back into place. She figured they could bake two pies at a time. That should keep them going until they could buy a proper wood stove for cooking. After that, she hoped the pies would be the moneymaker everyone thought they would be, and would get them through the season. Then they could buy steamship tickets to Seattle and head home in the fall. But she didn't know if they could make enough money to pay off the mortgage.

After seeing what little cooking the stampeders were doing on their own, Ellie understood why Rose and Mrs. Novak were so sure she could make money with pies. Bacon, biscuits, and beans got monotonous after a while. Even with dried apples instead of fresh ones, her pies would be the best eating most of the men would have had in a long time.

Her thoughts were interrupted by Billy's voice. "How much do you think we oughta charge for the pies?"

"Oh, maybe fifty cents a slice," she said as she gathered wood for their fire.

"That's not very much." He grabbed a handful of kindling. "We could probably get more."

"Johnny's place was charging fifty cents for a shot of whiskey. And it was cheap enough the men would come back for more, right? So they made a lot of money."

"I guess. They might buy a whole pie, too." Billy laid wood in the circle of rocks, left behind by a previous stampeder.

Ellie got the matches out of her pack. "I can light it, save your right hand a bit of work. So eight slices equals four dollars a pie, or we could give them a deal."

Her brother scratched around the stitches on his forehead, which made the leaden lump in her stomach return. "No, four bucks. We can't be mining the miners if we give them deals that are too good."

Ellie laughed at his savvy. Yes, he was definitely growing up.

AFTER A WEEK on the trail, Ellie and Billy were back on the boat to Skagway. The town looked as welcoming as an old friend, Ellie thought. She couldn't help smiling, watching the white tents shining in the sun in the little hamlet nestled between the mountains as the boat drew closer. Skagway looked so much better than the trail had, a relief after the hard, dirty work they'd left behind in the mountains.

Ellie and Billy plowed into the crowd at the beach, pushing through the mass of people on Broadway. She walked at Billy's side, not needing to hold his arm this time. No one paid them any attention on the boardwalk.

They entered the Alaska Saloon. Billy asked the bartender, "Is Johnny around?"

Instead of calling down the bar, the man walked over to them. "No, I'm sorry. His wife died a couple weeks ago and it broke his heart. He headed back to San Francisco."

Ellie's heart fluttered in her chest. "Rose?"

"I'm sorry, miss, she's passed on. Woman troubles." He indicated a stool. "Please, sit down. Can I get you something—a sarsaparilla?"

"No, no thank you." Ellie fingered her cameo and thought of the only other friends they had in town. "Sir, do you know where Duke Masterson and Dan Palmer are?"

"Yes, miss, they own the Frisco Saloon, on State Street—to your left."

"Thank you."

Ellie and Billy walked down the boardwalk through the crowd, past men in three-piece suits and bowlers, next to dusty stampeders right off the trail, like them. They turned down State Street and wound through the throng, past the bathhouse, general store, and bank.

The Frisco Saloon was a double-sized wall tent with a painted, wood sign over the entrance. Small, rough tables and benches filled the interior, and a larger table served as the bar. Ellie's heart leapt as she spotted Duke pouring drinks, laughing at something a customer said, and looking dapper in a new, silk waistcoat. His was the first shaven face she'd seen up close in a long time, and as handsome as she remembered it. Her cheeks grew hot as she thought of her appearance—no hat, hair in a simple braid, a borrowed blouse with sleeves too short for her, work pants, and muddy boots. What would he think of her now? She took a deep breath as she laid aside those thoughts. She and Billy needed help, and there was no time to dither about niceties.

"Duke," Billy called as they walked to the bar.

"Why, Billy." He broke into a smile and started to shake his right hand, but patted his shoulder instead when he saw the bandage. "And Ellie, good to see you." He shook her hand gently as his smile widened. "Please, sit down."

"We've been to the Alaska Saloon," Ellie said as she took the bench Duke pulled out for her.

"So you know about Johnny and Rose. He was so upset." Duke shook his head. "Too many memories. He had to get out of this place."

"What a shame," Billy said, eyes downcast.

"Listen, let me get you something to drink and we'll talk. A sarsaparilla? Coffee?"

"Coffee, please."

"I'll be right back."

As they watched, Duke—in one fluid motion—grabbed two mugs from a box under the bar, poured their coffee from the coffee pot on the wood stove in the middle of the tent, and then brought the mugs to their table.

He sat down next to Ellie, eyes locked on hers. "So, what's your news?"

"Well, we got up the trail, all the way to Lake Bennett," Ellie said, then paused.

"Good for you two," Duke said encouragingly.

Billy set his mug down. "Then our boat broke up in the rapids and we lost almost everything."

"Oh, no," Duke murmured.

"We're mostly all right," Ellie explained. "We got banged up a little. But our friend died." Tears slipped down her face, but she ignored them. "We lost most of our supplies and couldn't go on. So here we are, back in Skagway. We have to make money for Mama and the farm, and it's near the end of June already." Her tongue seemed to keep talking on its own. "Papa died of consumption last fall and Mama owes a mortgage on the farm equipment, so it's up to us to raise enough to pay it off. The corn's slow this year and we have to make some money, so we can keep the farm, and need to set up a pie business. There is a little money left, but I don't know where to set up or how to get started. We were going to ask Rose, but now she's gone. Can you help us, Duke?"

Duke handed her a handkerchief. "Of course I will."

"Sorry about crying. I feel so silly." She wiped the tears from her face.

"No, no, you're not silly at all. I think you're very strong and brave to make it to the rapids and back. Probably stronger than I am," he added with a sheepish grin. He patted her hand and let it linger there for a moment, and his warm touch brought a hot flush to her cheeks. "I tell you what, you sit here and enjoy your coffee—on the house of course. Dan is supposed to be back in"—he pulled out a gold pocket watch from his waistcoat pocket—"about ten minutes. Then one of us can watch the place here, and the other will get you going on a business location. All right?"

Billy nodded. "Yep. Thanks, Duke."

"Thank you, Duke." Ellie's gaze met his ever-blue eyes through her wet lashes, and she was surprised by the intensity of his smile.

"Glad to help." He beamed at her for a moment before going back to the bar.

Ellie stared out the tent entrance and wondered what just happened. She couldn't believe she, the strong one, cried in front of Duke. This emotional outburst was due to a combination of fatigue and nerves. She never cried around other people. Duke took it well, listened quietly, and gave his full attention to her. She would have expected him to be embarrassed or not know what to do with a woman's tears. But he did just what she would have wanted, if she'd thought about it ahead of time. He'd listened and treated her with respect.

Perhaps she had misjudged him in the beginning. He seemed to be a good man after all, and he did offer to help her, as she had hoped he would.

Ellie and Billy sipped their coffee and Ellie sent up a silent prayer for Rose and Johnny. Then she watched Duke at work.

His tall, masculine body was graceful as he wove his way among his customers, blue eyes sparkling as he smiled and greeted most men by name as they walked in. They all seemed happy to talk with him. Duke glanced at Ellie and Billy every few minutes, asked if they needed anything, refilled their coffee mugs, and worked his way around the tent, making sure everyone was satisfied. In his element here, as if he was the host of a grand party, he was a born bartender or salesman, Ellie decided, so at ease with people.

"Ellie," Billy whispered.

"Yes, Billy?"

"Do you like him better now?"

She laughed at how well her brother read her thoughts. "Yes, I do."

Soon, Dan arrived, looking even more portly than when they saw him at the beginning of the summer. He wore a different brown coat, and Ellie guessed that the partners' new clothes indicated their business was thriving.

Duke caught Dan at the door and leaned over to talk to him. Ellie supposed he was explaining everything. Moments later, Dan bustled to Ellie's table.

"Ellie, I'm so glad you're all right. Billy, good to see you."

"Hey, Dan."

Ellie smiled at him.

"Duke explained you need help getting settled. Let me take you around to a few people and we'll get you situated."

Ellie stood. "Thank you, Dan."

"You know"—Dan nodded toward the bar—"Duke would take you, but the new commissioner is a friend of mine. It's all in who you know around here." He winked.

By the end of the day, Ellie and Billy had their mended wall tent set up on Broadway Street, near Twelfth Avenue, basic supplies replenished, and dehydrated apples ready to boil in water. Billy constructed a safe place to build the fire and Ellie painted a sign that read, *Ellie's Pies*. They'd be open for business in the morning.

CHAPTER FOUR

A LIGHT RAIN pattered the top of the wall tent as Ellie pulled two pies out of the box oven. The tall limbs of the cedar trees above them kept the worst of the rain off the tent. The muddy street was busy with horses pulling wagons and men walking by, and the air smelled of wood smoke and apple pie.

"We'll be right with you," Billy called to the men in line as he quickly washed and dried plates and forks. Ellie was surprised but grateful he could work around his injury. "Okay, serving up more pie. Fifty cents a slice!"

Some dressed for the city, others fresh from the trail, all damp from the rain, Skagway residents and stampeders stood in line patiently. Men sat on the bench in front of the tent, paid their money, and ate pie as fast as Billy could serve it.

"Great pie, miss," a grubby miner said to Ellie through the open entrance of the wall tent. "Something I can do to help out here?"

"Ahh." Ellie thought of the woodpile shrinking behind the tent. "How about splitting some wood?"

"I can do that. Got an ax?"

"Next to the woodpile in back." She pointed. "Thank you."

"It's a privilege, after eating the best pie in Alaska." He flourished his battered felt hat at her, and then disappeared behind the tent.

"Reminds me of home," a man in a bowler hat said hoarsely. "Thank you, ma'am." With tears in his eyes, he shook her hand. "Want some help with those dishes?"

"Sure, thank you." She smiled and handed him the dishrag.

By noon, the line was a block long and Billy was sent to buy more pie tins, forks, and plates. Ellie made and baked pies while volunteers washed dishes, tended the fire, and built another bench for customers. Ellie's and Billy's pockets were heavy with coins, until someone found a cigar box to put the money in.

"Anything to help, miss," a tall man said.

Ellie knew the pies would be appreciated, but their popularity caught her by surprise. As she listened to the rhythmic chopping of wood, she raised her eyebrows at her brother, who grinned in reply.

ELLIE STOPPED MAKING pie when she ran out of apples.

"Sorry, folks, that's all until tomorrow morning."

Ellie and Billy sat on a bench and looked at the Jenkinson's Ideal Smokers box full of coins.

Ellie slapped at a mosquito. "I can't believe how fast those pies sold. And everybody wanted to help."

"What a day! What do we need to buy next, sis?"

"More pie makings, and how about a stove?"

"Sounds good to me." He pointed toward the bay. "They should have some in that general store down the street."

"Let's go shopping." She picked up the cash box and looked down at her dirty workpants. "How about some clean clothes and a bath, too?"

"Oh, that sounds good. Let's take the night off!" Billy rubbed his finger and a pang of guilt seized her stomach. At least they were making money. Maybe she wasn't a total failure.

Duke whistled as he sauntered up the boardwalk toward them, thumbs in the pockets of his silk waistcoat. "You two are the talk of the town today."

Billy laughed. "Hope in a good way."

"According to many, many people, you have the best pie in Alaska." He winked and indicated the empty tent. "Did you run out?"

Ellie grinned in triumph. "Yes, and we're taking the night off for shopping and a hot bath."

"Sounds like a well-deserved rest." Duke bowed and flourished his hat in an exaggerated salute. "May I take you two to dinner later this evening?"

"Sure," Billy said before Ellie could open her mouth. "If it's okay with Ellie."

"Well, thank you," Ellie accepted. "And could you recommend a good bathhouse?"

LATER THAT DAY, the stove was safely installed, and Ellie and Billy were clean. Ellie was glad she'd bought a new Gibson blouse and skirt, and styled her hair in a loose bun. The Burkhard House dining room was quite elegant, with its white table linens and china plates.

"Thank you for your invitation, Duke." Her heart pitter-pattered as she looked into his blue eyes.

"My pleasure." Duke smiled back with a twinkle in his eyes, and she admired his broad shoulders. He wore a clean, white shirt, black, silk waistcoat, and pressed, black pants. "Dan is holding the fort at the saloon, so I am free to socialize tonight."

"Are you making good money, too?" Billy asked. "Sorry," he added as Ellie shot daggers at him with a look. "Forgot polite people don't talk about money."

Duke waved the objection away. "No, it's all right. We're all here to make our fortunes. No sense in pretending otherwise. Yes, I expect we'll close up shop at the end of summer with a tidy sum."

Billy grinned. "I'm surprised at how much we got today. Might have the mortgage paid off by then, too."

"Well, I'm glad to hear it," Duke said as the waiter stopped to take their order. "Three of your daily specials, please."

"Yes, sir." He nodded and disappeared into the kitchen.

Duke dropped his voice a notch. "Daily specials are whatever the best food is that day, so it'll be fresh and delicious."

"Thank you." Ellie sipped her water. "What surprised me today is how much the customers wanted to help. They washed dishes, chopped wood—all kinds of chores."

"It is due to your beauty and charm, my dear, as well as your pies." Duke toasted her with his water glass. As he smiled, his dark goatee framed his full, pink lips nicely. Ellie wondered what it would be like to kiss those lips, then scolded herself for the thought. She would not lower her standards and give in to unladylike behavior.

"And the fact that you're a good woman in this town doesn't hurt any," Billy added. "I heard people say you remind them of their daughter, or sister, or their sweetheart back home."

"It seemed ungracious to turn them away, especially when they offered and we could use the help." She indicated Billy's bandaged hand.

"You're a practical woman, Ellie Webster. Besides, I think they enjoyed doing something for you. Some were bragging at the saloon about it. If it continues at this rate, you'll have men competing to help you with chores."

Ellie wondered what she'd started. "Oh, dear. I hadn't anticipated that."

"Oh, it'll be fine. There's not much amusement in this town that doesn't cost a great deal. You'll give them a little diversion from their daily routine."

"Garden salad," the waiter announced as he placed a small plate of lettuce, carrots, and onion on each place setting.

Ellie sighed as she gazed at the sight. "I haven't seen fresh vegetables in so long."

"Bon appétit." Duke waved his fork at them then started in on his own plate. They ate in silence, Ellie savoring every bite. Who knew that a piece of lettuce could be so precious? She guessed the customers felt the same about her pies.

"Hey, you're Miss Ellie." A bald man came up to them and shook her hand. "Wonderful pie."

"Why, thank you."

"Enjoy your meal, miss."

"Thank you, you too," she said as he left.

Duke winked at her. "I'm eating with a celebrity."

Her cheeks turned hot. "Oh, don't."

"I guess you kind of are, sis." Her brother grinned. She focused on the stitches on his forehead and made a mental note to find a doctor to take them out.

"Let's talk about Duke for a change." Ellie maneuvered the conversation. "So, Duke, what do you like to do when you're not working?"

"Oh, back in San Francisco, I listen to music. Not much of that here in Skagway, but sometimes we get a good Irish tenor or songstress come through. I mainly play cards or read."

"I haven't seen a book in ages," Ellie said. "Is there a library here?"

"No, but the YMCA has a reading room in the church building. What do you like to read, Ellie?"

"Just about anything I can find. My favorite right now is the Sherlock Holmes mysteries."

"They are fun, aren't they? And I bet you're clever enough to figure out the solutions before you finish the story."

She noticed his lips again and glanced away.

"Roasted salmon with potatoes," the waiter announced and served each of them a plate.

"See that man at the door there, with the beard?" Duke asked in a quiet voice.

A tall, young man with dark hair and a full beard, dressed in a suit and broad-brimmed hat, stood near the entrance.

"That's Jeff Smith—Soapy Smith," Duke explained.

"The telegraph man?" Billy asked after they watched Smith leave.

"Yes, and he also has connections with most of the money in this town," Duke added. "I play cards with him once in a while."

She sniffed. "Why spend time with someone like that?"

Duke smiled ruefully. "You can pick your friends, but not your neighbors. Sometimes, it's best to try to get along."

Ellie hoped she wouldn't have to deal with the likes of Soapy Smith.

"Good salmon," Billy commented.

"And good company." Duke toasted Ellie again with a warm smile in his eyes.

The blood ran into her cheeks when she met his glance. "Thank you."

"SO HOW WAS dinner last night?" Dan asked as he wiped down the bar.

"Nice," Duke said lightly as he loaded wood into the stove. "Thanks for working without me."

"You're welcome. So, did she enjoy it?"

"Yes. Said she hadn't had fresh vegetables in a long time." Duke smiled at the tent wall, remembering the way Ellie had sighed over her salad.

"And you were charming?"

He laughed at his partner's persistence. "Well, she didn't say that, but I tried."

Opening a box of beer bottles under the bar, Dan paused. "Ellie's the only girl you've been interested in since we've been here, so I'm a little curious."

"She's lovely and she's got spirit. And I think she's decided I'm a nice person now. So we'll have to see what happens."

"Okay, we'll see. She is something," Dan agreed.

"You're not looking, too, are you?" Duke's voice came out sharper than he'd intended.

Dan laughed. "No, no, she's all yours, partner. Don't worry about that."

"Sorry." Duke wondered at his pang of jealousy. It wouldn't be like Dan to steal a woman Duke was interested in seeing, although Ellie didn't seem eager to spend time with any man in particular.

She was so keen on making money for her farm back home. He felt lucky she'd agreed to his dinner invitation and was glad she had. Ellie was a lovely young lady, honest, like a breath of fresh air after a rain shower, and not a pretentious bone in her body. With Ellie, what you saw was what was there.

He imagined loosening her brown, wavy hair out of that bun and watching it cascade down her back. He'd kissed her hand as tenderly as he could when he walked her home that evening, fancying it was her soft, full lips. Before, he'd admired her from afar, but now that he'd spent some time with her, he wanted to get to know her better.

Duke longed to understand Ellie's thoughts and emotions, and hold her in his arms. One dinner, with Billy as chaperone, was only the beginning. He yearned for Ellie Webster in a way he hadn't any woman before. And he wanted her to love him as he was starting to love her.

ELLIE PULLED FOUR pies out of the new cook stove and set them to cool on the table a customer had built that morning. The tent was becoming a little crowded, with the living quarters in the back half and the pie making business in the front. Perhaps it was time to buy a bigger tent. But that would mean less money for Mama. She glanced around the makeshift living space. If they organized their belongings carefully, they could rough it for a couple months, like Duke and Dan were doing with their saloon.

Hands on her hips, Ellie gazed unseeing at the white canvas wall of the tent, thinking about Duke's goodbye last night. He'd kissed her hand in the most gentle manner. As she stood there, she could almost feel his lips on her knuckles.

He could be very sweet. She enjoyed spending time with him. But why did he give her so many compliments? Was it because there were few good women in town and he lacked female company, or did he really like her? It was hard to tell. But, she supposed, it didn't matter, since they'd only see each other for a few more weeks. At the end of the summer, she'd go home to the farm and he'd head back to San Francisco.

She sighed and started to mix another batch of piecrust dough.

"Can I help you with the stove wood, Miss Ellie?" a youth asked, Stetson hat in hand.

"Sure, we could use some more. The ax is in back."

"I was going to do that," a tall man in overalls said indignantly.

"Sir, can you help me with the dishes?" she asked.

"Oh, all right."

"Please fill that bucket with hot water first. The pot of water on the stove should be warm enough by now. Then there'll be plates to wash."

"Yes, miss."

All day, Ellie baked pies, Billy served and directed the crowd, and men volunteered to help. Ellie did her best to deflect any conflicts and find something for everyone to do. She never dreamed she'd be in this position, ordering men to do chores in what amounted to her own kitchen.

Back home, she ordered Billy around, and maybe a field hand or two at harvest time, but here in Skagway, men hung onto her every word and practically jumped when she told them to do something. It gave her a sense of power she'd never had before.

She could almost hear Mama's voice telling her not to let it go to her head. As she watched men argue over chopping wood, Ellie tried not to smile too much, but it tickled her fancy that they liked to help her. Ellie knew Mama would laugh if she could see the scene.

She wiped her hands on her apron and smoothed the long skirt she'd bought yesterday. People were nice here, even without the comforts of home, made do, and created their own amusements. Ellie listened to the men singing *There'll Be a Hot Time In The Old Town Tonight* as they waited in line for pie.

A BREEZE STIRRED the leaves on the trees after the rain ended. Ellie served a piece of pie to a white-haired gentleman. "Here you are, sir."

"Thank you, miss." He tipped his hat as he took the plate.

Something about his face was familiar. "Haven't I seen you before?"

"Yes, miss. I was here yesterday. Just had to have another piece of pie before I left town."

"Well, thank you, sir. How kind of you."

The pop from a gunshot down the street made them jump.

"Don't worry, Miss Ellie, that's only someone whooping it up," a miner assured her.

The man next to him huffed. "Wish they'd do it without wasting good ammunition."

"It does seem wasteful," she agreed, her heart still racing. She waited for the next person in line to step up. To her surprise, it was a boy about seven years old. "Hello. Do you want some pie?"

"Yes, please. I'm Robert Hickock. My ma and pa run the hotel across the street." He pointed to the building with the white, flat facade sitting kitty-corner across the street from Ellie's pie tent. "They want me to tell you that you are welcome to stop by anytime you need something."

"Well, thank you! That's very nice of them and you."

"You're welcome, Miss Ellie. Good pie," he said through a mouthful.

Ellie smiled at the hotel's windows, but didn't see any sign of the boy's mother. It was nice to know there was another woman in town she could talk to. It'd been ages since she'd had women talk with anyone.

"Um, miss?" the next man in line reminded her she had customers waiting.

"Oh, sorry, here you are." She served the last piece of pie in the tin.

"Thanks, miss."

Ellie pulled the next pie toward her on the table and cut it into pieces. "Okay, ready for the next customer."

Billy appeared from behind the tent. "I can get the next one."

"Then I'll load up the stove."

A cowboy jumped up from the bench. "No, wait! Allow me, Miss Ellie."

She laughed. "All right, I'll start the next batch of pies." It was getting hard to keep up with all the volunteers.

THAT NIGHT, BILLY and Ellie finished cleaning up from the day's work—what hadn't already been done by their customers—and walked across to the Skagway Hotel. Thank goodness the rain had stopped, so Ellie and Billy were dry except for the mud their boots picked up from the street.

The lobby was decorated with red-flocked wallpaper and dark walnut furniture. A couple of men sat next to the wood stove, smoking cigars. Robert Hickock perched on a stool at the front desk, but he hopped down as Ellie and Billy approached him.

"Hi, Miss Ellie." He offered his hand in a grown up handshake.

She took it gently. "Hi, Robert. This is my brother, Billy."

Ellie turned as she heard someone running down the stairs.

"That's my little sister Lizzie, and my ma." Robert waved toward the little girl in a pinafore and brown curls, a little smaller than her brother. The pretty lady behind her had curly hair swept up in a bun. She smoothed her white apron over her brown, calico dress and stretched her hand out to Ellie.

"Call me Ada." The woman smiled, dimples showing in her cheeks. "My husband, Tom, is away right now. Please, sit down." Ada indicated the stuffed sofa and chairs in the lobby near them. Ellie ignored the men staring at them from the wood stove. The adults sat down while the children stood by their mother. Ellie and Billy admired the portraits on the wall.

"We got our pictures taken last month," Robert explained. "There's a photographer place on the next street over."

Billy nodded at the little boy. "Very nice."

"Can I get you something to drink? Tea?" Ada asked.

"Tea would be lovely, thank you." Ellie hadn't had tea since her time with the Novaks. A twinge of guilt grabbed her heart as she thought of sitting here, safe and sound, while Bobby Joe was dead.

"I'll get it!" Robert said.

"I can help!" Lizzie ran after him as he left the room. The adults smiled after the children.

"So where are you from?" Ada asked.

"Nebraska," Ellie answered.

"Really? Tom's from Montana."

Billy grinned. "Hey, that's practically next door."

"Isn't that something? I bet you miss the plains, too."

"Oh, yes. The mountains here are beautiful, but I'm used to big sky," Billy confessed.

Ada nodded. "Very different here. But, like you said, our mountains have their own beauty. And it's so green here."

"That's what I like the best," Ellie said.

Billy took the cup of tea that Lizzie held out to him—tipped precariously to one side—before it spilled.

Lizzie smiled shyly at Billy, while Robert delivered tea to Ellie and his mother, before sitting on the floor by her mother's chair.

The warm cup of tea felt good in Ellie's tired hands.

Robert grinned up at her. "Anybody need sugar or cream? It's actually canned milk," he added apologetically.

"No, thank you."

"I'll take a little sugar," Billy requested, holding the teacup in his left hand. Seeing the right one with its bandage sent another leaden weight to the bottom of Ellie's stomach.

"Sure." Robert ran out of the room and returned with the sugar bowl and spoon.

"It looks like your pie tent is doing well," Ada observed.

"Yes. We're pretty busy."

"Those men love your pies. Has Soapy Smith contacted you?"

"About what?"

Ada shook her head. "Maybe your business is too small to be of interest to him. Never mind."

Before Ellie could ask further questions, Billy turned to Ada. "Are there many children in Skagway?"

Ada answered, "Some, maybe twenty, whose folks are here. They're starting up a school."

Ellie set her teacup on the saucer. "That would be nice."

"Yes." Ada's dimples deepened as she laughed at Robert's wrinkled nose. "But Robert was hoping to skip school this year, so he's not happy about it."

"I bet the children find lots to do around here to amuse themselves," Ellie said, changing the subject.

Robert grinned. "Oh, yes. There's fishing, and climbing trees, and berries to pick sometimes."

"And tag, and ball, and jump rope," Lizzie added. "Maybe we can play sometime?"

"Thanks for the invitation, but we're working most of the day."

Billy yawned, and Ellie thought it was probably time for the children to go to bed. "My, it's getting late. We should go."

"Feel free to stop by anytime. Maybe you can meet Tom next time." Ada stood.

"We'd like that."

"Thanks for the tea." Billy put his hat on at the door. "Good to meet you."

"Don't be strangers."

"Good night!"

Ellie and Billy walked back to the tent. As Billy loaded the stove with wood, Ellie thought about how grateful she was for a warm place to sleep. The evenings were cool, although the sun still shone when they went to bed.

Billy yawned as he got into bed. "Nice to see a family out here."

"Yes, good to see children again," Ellie agreed as she lay down on her cot. It was wonderful to lie down. The pie business was harder than she expected. But it was still better than trudging up the Scales.

Ellie rolled on to her side and thought of Ada and her children. Ada looked less worn out than the wives back in Nebraska did. Perhaps married life was easier in a town. But there were still problems. Ellie thought of Rose. So much could happen to a woman, from the time she said her vows to the moment she took her last breath.

She didn't know if she'd get married one day.

ELLIE ROLLED OUT pie dough as she listened to customers talking.

"Did you go all the way to Eldorado Creek?" a young man about Billy's age asked a grizzled old miner.

"Yep, along with hundreds of others. All the best places were claimed. But I went in with another guy on a claim up on Willow Crick, in the hills."

"Have any luck?"

"Found some gold dust after a couple months of breaking our backs. It is hard, hard work."

"So then what happened?"

"I got tired of pannin', and diggin', and sluicin'. The gold fever died out in me, I reckon. Left it all to Jim and headed back here. I can make more working for the packers in a week than I did up there in two months."

"Gosh." The younger man sounded disappointed.

Another man waved his fork in the young man's face. "Learn from us, sonny. It ain't all paved with gold up there. Just hard work and bad luck."

Maybe Mrs. Novak was right, Ellie thought as she sprinkled cinnamon and sugar on the apples. *We are better off down here in town.*

The next man in line had shaggy, brown hair, reminding her of Bobby Joe. As she served him a piece of pie, she tried to swallow the lump in her throat and smile. She pushed the thought of Bobby Joe out of her mind for the moment—better to stay focused on the present. Her job was to make money and take care of Billy. Sentiment would have to wait.

Duke poured a mug of coffee for a man in a three-piece suit. Another good day for the saloon. And he felt content tonight.

Ellie's face came to his mind. He cherished having her in his life, even if he didn't see her often. That's what was missing before—Ellie. And now, if he played his cards right, he had a chance with her. If this summer went right, he'd have bushels of money and the love of a good woman by August. Duke wanted that to happen more than anything. He hoped Ellie would feel the same.

"Over here, mister," a customer called.

"Yes, sir. What'll you have?"

"Whiskey."

"Coming right up."

Soapy Smith came into the tent and headed for the bar. He and Dan exchanged a few words, then Dan handed him some money. It was part of doing business in Skagway, paying Soapy periodically to keep the man pacified. Duke didn't like it, but it was a fact of life here.

CHAPTER FIVE

The tall, dusty miner smiled at Billy, but the smile disappeared as he patted his pockets. "It's gone! Somebody stole my poke!"

"It wasn't one of us. I've been standing behind you the whole time and I didn't see anything," Ralph, a portly customer wearing a bowler hat, said.

Ellie sighed. "Now think a minute. Where were you before this?"

"Um, Jeff's Parlor."

One man harrumphed in disgust and several shook their heads.

"Just had a quick beer before I came here."

Ralph asked as if talking to a child, "Didn't anybody tell you not to go in there?"

"Shouldn't go in there," his tall friend, Jim, said behind him.

"No, I only got to Skagway this morning," the miner said, dumbfounded.

Ellie took off her apron and tossed it on the table. "Being new in town is no reason to be preyed upon. Let's go take care of this."

"Ellie, are you crazy?" Billy said. "You can't just go—"

"What's your name?" Ellie asked the miner, ignoring Billy.

"Frank Thompson."

"Let's go see Jeff Smith, Frank Thompson." Ellie raised her hand and he held up the crook of his arm so she could rest it there. They walked down the street—Ellie with a determined gait, Frank Thompson barely keeping up with her. Billy and several customers followed a few feet behind.

They sailed through the doorway of the small saloon and Ellie steered Frank toward the bar. Soapy Smith, wearing his broad-rimmed hat, looked down at Ellie.

"Can I help you?" he said as he tipped his hat, amusement in his eyes.

"Mr. Smith, this gentleman was here in your establishment and lost his poke." Ellie smiled at Smith. "I know you'd want to do the right thing by helping him find it."

Smith drawled, "Are you accusing me of running a shady operation? Miss, I wouldn't—"

Several of the pie customers started to bristle and draw closer to them.

"No, of course not." Ellie smiled again and shook her head. "I'm sure you honest folks would have noticed the poke by now and be ready to hand it over to the original owner." She turned to her escort. "Now, Mr. Thompson, what did this poke look like?"

"It's a small, leather pouch, had about twenty dollars worth of nuggets in it."

With a wave, Ellie addressed the other men in the room. "So has anyone seen it?"

The bartender coughed. "Um, I think it's right here." He pulled out a sack from behind the bar and handed it to him.

"Thank you." Frank Thompson gazed at the poke in his hands, as if it had appeared by magic.

"Now, I think we should be going. Thank you for your help," Ellie addressed the bartender. "And you, Mr. Smith."

Soapy tipped his hat again as Ellie sailed out the door with her entourage. Back in the street, the men started toward the pie tent, laughing and slapping each other on the back.

Ralph boasted, "Did you see that look on Soapy's face? He couldn't do nothing 'cept let Miss Ellie have her say."

"Boy, Miss Ellie, that was a great thing you did!" Billy's friend Harry said.

Ellie shook her head at her men. "Thank you, but I think that'll only work once. You boys better stay out of that place, and spread the word."

"Yes, ma'am, we sure will."

"Ellie Webster, did I see you coming out of Jeff's Parlor?" Duke Masterson glared down at her, chest heaving, as he fell into step beside her.

"Oh, hello, Duke. I was helping this man get his money back."

"Ellie, you can't just waltz into—" He stopped walking, as if he realized what she said. "What happened?"

"Frank Thompson here had his poke stolen while he was in there and discovered it missing when he got to our place. So I went in to Jeff's Parlor with him, and explained that Mr. Thompson lost it, and said I was sure that someone had found the poke and would return it to its rightful owner."

Duke's brow furrowed. "And what happened?"

"The bartender handed it to Frank, we thanked him and Soapy, and left. Except I didn't call him Soapy, of course."

"Soapy was there? Do you realize what a dangerous thing you just did?"

"Dangerous? They wouldn't do anything to a decent woman in public, would they?"

"No, but you just lost him some money. He won't forget that."

"Oh, Duke, you don't need to worry about me. I can take care of myself."

Duke shook his head. "I knew you'd say that." He sighed then looked into her eyes imploringly. "Please, Ellie, if Soapy Smith ever contacts you, come get me. Let me help, all right?"

Was she in danger? She didn't understand why this was so important to Duke, but maybe there was something she didn't know about Soapy Smith. "All right, if it will make you feel better. I'll send for you if Soapy comes around."

"Or if he contacts you in any way," Duke pressed.

"Yes, I will. Now, would you like some pie?"

"No, thanks. I'm headed to the bank. Anything I can do for you?"

"No, thank you, Duke."

Duke turned to stride back down the street and Ellie noticed that Billy had started serving pie again. She tied her apron around her waist.

Frank Thompson placed two gold nuggets in Billy's hand.

"Oh, Frank, this is too much," Billy protested.

"That's for the pie and the help. Think of them as souvenirs of Alaska. Thank you, Miss Ellie."

"You're welcome. Now watch that poke more closely."

"Yes, ma'am, I will."

That evening, as they finished cleaning up, Ellie scratched her red hands, irritated from all the washing and cooking. Maybe Ada would know of a remedy that might help. She'd ask her later.

Ellie looked up at Billy and saw how tired he appeared. Maybe he needed a diversion from all this work. And they required a doctor to look at his stitches and right hand.

"Let's take a short walk. See if we can find the doctor's office."

"Okay, sis." Billy grabbed his felt hat and tied up the tent flap as she put her shawl around her shoulders.

Ellie and Billy picked their way around the mud puddles to the boardwalk and walked away from the bay, toward the forest. Wagons rolled by on the muddy street. The scent of horses and mud filled Ellie's nose.

"Packers! Get your gear packed down the trail!" a burly man shouted. Another man paused to check on his rates.

A pie customer stopped them on the boardwalk, an older man from town in a pinstripe suit. "Why, it's Miss Ellie. Billy."

"Hello. Is it Sid?" Ellie said, trying to get his name right.

"Yes, ma'am." He puffed up at her remembering his name. "It was nice what you did for Frank Thompson today. Out for a stroll?"

"Yes, we are," Billy answered.

"Well, have a nice evening." Sid tipped his hat and went on his way.

The racket of hammers on wood announced a new building going up across the street. Ellie and Billy stopped in front of the Skagway News office.

"Look, Billy, they have a newspaper." Ellie drew them inside.

"Not any newspaper. The best in the territory," the whiskered man at the desk said. "Would you like to buy a copy?"

Ellie knew it was an unnecessary expense, but she was curious to see what was happening back home.

"Yes, please. Any news of the war?"

"Right here, on the bottom of page one." He pointed it out. "We cover local news mostly, but there's some national, too."

Billy tucked the paper under his arm after Ellie handed it to him. "We'll read it later. Thank you, sir." Ellie smiled at the editor.

He tipped his hat. "Thank you, miss."

The next two businesses were saloons, bigger than the Frisco or Jeff's Parlor. A ragtime piano played and scantily-clad women ducked into the building as Ellie and Billy walked by. Ellie was glad that Duke and Dan's place was more genteel. She hadn't seen any saloon girls in the Frisco.

A group of men sat in chairs in front of a hotel. They stood and tipped their hats when she approached. "Evening, Miss Ellie."

"Good evening."

A fat man nodded. "It sure was nice what you did for Frank Thompson. Let us know if you need anything."

"We appreciate that." Word got around quickly. "Do you know of a doctor in town?"

"Yes, Miss Ellie, there's Doc Loman about two blocks that way."

"Thank you. We need to get Billy checked over." She indicated his bandage and he blushed.

"Didn't need to say that," Billy bristled next to her as they walked away.

She supposed it was his emerging male pride, not wanting to appear weak. "Don't be so sensitive. It's obvious you have an injury, with the stitches and bandage. No shame in that."

He huffed but didn't say anything else.

A raven cawed overhead as it swooped and perched on a nearby tree. Following its path with her eyes, Ellie stared at the mountains. Craggy, white peaks shone in the sunlight. They stopped and enjoyed the view for a moment.

Doctor Loman's place was nearby. A sign in the window advertised his office hours, which they had missed.

"We'll have to come by during the day to get you checked out."

Billy yawned.

"It's late, let's head back," Ellie suggested.

"All right."

As the breeze picked up, Ellie drew her shawl around her. A broad-shouldered man with dark hair walked ahead of them, reminding her of Duke. She wondered what he was doing now— probably pouring drinks for someone, or laughing at a customer's joke. His dazzling blue eyes came to her mind and she smiled at the thought of them.

Careful Ellie, she told herself, you're starting to get sweet on him. *You're here to do a job, make money for Mama, and escort Billy safely back home. Don't be distracted by a man, even if he is handsome and caring.*

She patted her brother's arm. "We'll need to buy more pie ingredients tomorrow."

"I can go to the store after I get the stove going in the morning."

"Thanks. That'll be fine. Or I can mind the stove."

"Whatever you like. You're the boss," Billy grumped.

It was true. Ellie liked being in charge and in control of things. It would take some getting used to when they got back home and she had to give that up. Or maybe she wouldn't stay on the farm. That was something to think about later. But, for now, it was nice to be the boss.

She closed the tent flap and took off her shawl. "Tired?"

"Yep."

"Go ahead and get ready for bed. I'll stay up a bit and read the newspaper."

"Okay, tell me about anything big going on."

"I will." She scanned the page. "Looks like they're still fighting in Cuba."

THE NEXT MORNING, the line at their tent was even longer than before, thick and a block-and-a-half long by the time they started serving pie.

Billy's grin was wide. "Wow, look at that. Should be a good day."

"We all heard about what you and Ellie did for Frank," the first man in line said. "Figured we oughta support a lady who stands up to Soapy Smith."

Ellie answered, "I just did what any of you would do for someone in need."

The man waved his fork at her. "No, ma'am, you did what any of us *should have done.* There's a difference."

"Got more guts than most men. Thanks for sticking up for us little folks," the next customer said. "And this pie is delicious."

"She's pretty, tough, and she cooks like an angel," another man said. Someone down the line started singing *Queen of Angels*.

"Thank you." Ellie smiled as she measured a cup of flour. It was nice that the men appreciated what she did. It would also help her pie tent.

She liked this business thing. She wondered how much she could make in one week, at this rate, and thought it through as she added lard to the flour.

If she made four pies an hour and sold them for eight hours a day, that equaled thirty-two pies multiplied by eight pieces, times fifty cents…

That was one hundred and twenty-eight dollars a day—more money than she'd ever seen at one time before. And if she was a little faster she could make more pies than that. At that rate, they could make enough money for the mortgage. Maybe even more than enough.

"Could I chop some wood for you, Miss Ellie?" Frank Thompson interrupted her thoughts.

"I guess, if you'd like to. The ax is over there."

"Anything to help a friend," Frank added as he tipped his dusty hat and disappeared around the corner of the tent.

Ellie rolled out the pie dough and thought that Frank had a pleasant smile, but his was nothing compared to Duke's. She saw Duke in her mind's eye as he appeared to her yesterday. He'd been so earnest about her contacting him. Perhaps he really cared for her.

She didn't see why he had to get upset about the Soapy Smith situation at the time, but looking at all the men in line this morning, maybe Duke had a point. If they all told people that a little lady beat Soapy, Soapy might have a bone to pick with her. It would be a good idea to lie low for a while until the talk faded away.

"Sis, is there more pie ready?" Billy called.

"Coming right up."

DUKE WATCHED AS Dan laughed at a customer's joke. He was sure having fun with the saloon. And Duke was too, come to think of it. The place was busy enough to be more than profitable. Of course, it was hard to go wrong with a drinking establishment in a mining town. They picked a perfect way to get rich in a hurry.

"Bartender, another round," a customer called from the other end of the bar. Duke grabbed a bottle of whiskey and walked over to him.

"Miss Ellie is her name," the man was saying to his companion. "She makes pies down the street here, walks right up to Soapy and says, 'This man lost his poke in here and I'm sure you've found it by now. So you can give it back to its rightful owner,' and then she bats her big brown eyes at him."

Duke poured the drinks but lingered to hear more.

"Really? What did Soapy do?" the companion asked.

"Nothing. The bartender gives her the poke and she says, 'Thank you, Mr. Smith,' and walks out."

The companion laughed. "Just like that? Well, I gotta buy me a piece of pie tomorrow."

Duke's face was hot and he clenched the bottle in his fist. He fought the sudden urge to punch the man, forcing himself to walk to the other end of the bar. They weren't trying to cut in on his girl, he reasoned, only going over what happened yesterday. But that's exactly what he was afraid people would do. If Soapy Smith thought people were making fun of him because of Ellie, he might make things difficult for her. Or even put an end to her pie stand.

Duke recalled Ellie crying in his saloon her first day back from the trail, and vowed he'd never see her cry again.

He took a deep breath. *You've got to think clearly here. What can you actually do? She's an independent lady, so don't go ruffle her feathers. If you approach her the wrong way, she'll turn you away and you can't do anything about it.*

Duke smiled as he poured a drink for a plump man in a three-piece suit. Then he went back to the monologue in his head. *At least Ellie promised to let you know if Soapy contacted her. She likes your company and enjoyed the dinner, so ask her out again. Take her to the concert Friday.*

He wasn't sure if he was trying to protect her or just finding an excuse to spend time with her. But either way, he needed to see Ellie. Soon.

"I HEAR THERE'S a new wharf going in," Billy said that night. "Want to go see it tonight?"

She thought of Duke's concern last time she saw him. "No, I think we better stay home. We don't want to call too much attention to ourselves. It might get Soapy Smith upset if he thinks we're rubbing his face in what happened."

He scratched his stitches. "I guess that makes sense. Don't want to make him mad."

"But I do want to get you into the doctor's office. We need to have those stitches and your hand examined. We'll stop work a little early tomorrow."

ELLIE DRIED THE last pie pan and untied her apron.

Billy held up his arm gallantly so she could rest her hand on the crook of his elbow. He seemed more sure of himself nowadays. They started down the boardwalk toward the bay.

"Pretty day, isn't it?" her brother asked. The afternoon was warm with a bit of a breeze, and the sun shone on the mountains.

"Yes, it is." They stopped to read a poster on a fence, advertising an Irish tenor performance.

"It says he's sung for the King of England. Want to go?" Billy asked.

"No, we better keep making pies. I figured out that we can make one hundred and twenty-eight dollars a day, if we work eight hours a day."

"That's a lot of money."

"We could get even more if we add an hour or two."

"Gosh, yes."

They continued down the street past the barbershop and the post office. Ralph and Jim tipped their hats.

"Afternoon, Miss Ellie. Billy."

"Afternoon," Jim echoed.

"Hello. Do you live here in town?"

"Yes, Miss Ellie. We work at Buxton's store over that way."

"Over that way." Jim pointed.

A man stumbled into Ellie, and then grinned as he looked into her face. "Hey, pretty lady, want to make some time?"

Jim shoved him aside just as Ralph opened his mouth to address the drunk. "Don't you know who this is? This is Miss Ellie, from the pie tent."

"Oh, excuse me." The man took his hat off.

Billy glared down at him. "Don't you be talking to my sister that way."

"Gentlemen, please," Ellie called as she stepped between them. "Be reasonable."

"Only trying to help," Ralph said.

"Thank you." Ellie took Billy's arm and walked down the boardwalk, passing a photography studio. "You didn't need to make a scene, Billy."

"Well, we can't have drunks accosting you either," Billy defended himself.

"Remember, we want to lie low for a little while."

"Oh." Billy nodded.

The livery stable smelled of hay and horses. She thought of the barn at home and wondered how the stable owners got hay in Skagway.

A gunshot in the saloon across the street made them both jump and Ellie squeezed Billy's arm. "I wish they wouldn't do that."

"Part of living in a boom town," Billy answered.

"I suppose so." But she wondered if anyone got hurt from all that gunplay. She couldn't have Billy shot on top of everything else that had gone wrong.

They turned into Doctor Loman's office. He looked like a doctor in an advertisement—a kindly middle-aged man with a bit of a paunch.

"You can call me Doc. Let's take a look at you," he said to Billy as he ushered him into his examination room.

Ellie's stomach twisted as she imagined all the things that might go wrong with Billy's injuries. But, within minutes, the doctor and Billy came out of the room smiling.

"Everything is healing okay. Come back in a couple weeks or so," Doc said.

They continued on down the street and stopped at the edge of the bay. A crew was building a new wharf next to the old one. The sun sparkled on the water and a steamship chugged its way up the canal toward town, hugging the shore where the green mountains met the sea. Ellie didn't know what was more beautiful, the mountains or the water.

Billy sighed. "Wish Mama could see this place."

"Yes, me too." She thought again of her promises to Mama, and she glanced at Billy's right hand, which had a clean bandage on the last two fingers.

They enjoyed the scene for a few minutes, then Ellie patted her brother on the shoulder and they turned back. "Guess we've seen most of the town now."

"There are a couple more streets on each side, but this is the main one," Billy answered. "I wonder what it would be like to live in a big city, like San Francisco."

Ellie laughed. "Noisy? I don't know, but perhaps we will one day. I never thought we'd be in Alaska, so who knows what'll happen next."

"Yep, who knows?"

Before this year, Ellie never thought of travelling outside their county. Now here she was, thousands of miles away, running her own business, and enjoying it.

Suddenly Ellie didn't want to live the rest of her life on a farm. The world seemed to offer a lot more opportunities than she'd expected. She'd have to think about them. But when? She kept crowding out thoughts of Bobby Joe, her future, Duke, things that didn't involve her goals of making money, and getting Billy home safely. It was like being on the Golden Stairs again, concentrating on placing one foot in front of the other. Eventually, she'd have to think about those things. And she wasn't sure she'd like her conclusions.

DUKE WAS AT their tent when they returned, all spruced up and wearing his black, silk waistcoat. "Evening, Miss Ellie. Billy."

"Why, Duke, I thought you'd be at your saloon." Ellie shook the hand he offered, hers fitting easily inside his.

"I was, but I stepped out for a moment. Ellie, I apologize if I meddled too much yesterday, but I was worried about your safety."

"Oh, that's all right. Thank you for your concern."

"Has Soapy contacted you?"

"No, he hasn't. But I'll let you know if he does."

"Yes, please do. There's an Irish tenor coming to town. Would you be interested in attending the concert with me?"

Her heart wanted to say yes, but she knew she shouldn't. "No, thank you. We really need to focus on the pies for a while."

Duke's face fell as he heard her answer.

"Maybe another time," Ellie added to soften the blow.

He brightened. "I'll take a rain check then. See you later, Billy." He tipped his hat then strode down the street.

"Bye," Billy called after him as he left.

Ellie untied the tent entrance and slipped inside. Billy followed her.

"You know, sis, I think he really likes you."

She couldn't help smiling as she answered, "Oh, probably not. He's just glad to know a nice girl in town." But inwardly, she wondered if it was more than that. Part of her hoped he'd invite her out again, even though she should be concentrating on the pie business. Something about Duke Masterson made it hard to set him aside completely.

DUKE FOUND HIMSELF taking the long way back to the saloon, wanting to think for a minute before returning to the bustle. Ellie seemed glad to see him, even let her fingers linger when shaking his hand. She said no to his invitation, but she'd left the door open when she'd said *maybe another time*. Did she feel something for him? Hard to tell for sure. But at least he could keep an eye on her, and help her if the situation with Soapy Smith became a problem.

Even if she didn't love him, Duke would do his best to protect her. He'd have to think about how to do that. But maybe, one day, she'd grow to love him. He hoped so.

And he'd do his best to make it happen.

CHAPTER SIX

"I THINK THAT'LL do it for the night," Ellie said to Billy a few days later as she dried the last of the pie pans.

"Hi, Duke," Billy called from the front of the tent.

"Good evening," Duke answered.

Ellie's heart beat faster as she smoothed her hair and strode to the doorway. "Hello!"

"Good evening, Miss Ellie," Duke said as he kissed her hand.

"My," she said.

He lingered for a moment before releasing her hand. "You're looking well, as usual." As he rose to his full height he smiled down at her, his clear blue eyes glittering.

"Thank you." Her cheeks grew hot.

"I think I'll go check on the stove wood," Billy excused himself before disappearing behind the tent.

"Please, sit down." Ellie indicated the bench. "We have one piece of pie left, would you like it?"

"Yes, thank you," Duke said. Ellie got the pie and brought it out to him. He waited until Ellie sat on the other bench first before sitting down.

"I enjoyed having dinner with you the other night." Ellie felt her cheeks flush again.

"One reason I stopped by was to thank you for coming. Should have said it earlier, but I enjoyed it, too." Duke smiled and looked into her eyes, holding her gaze for a moment before Ellie glanced away.

"Excellent pie," Duke said between bites.

"I have some coffee left over from dinner—" she offered.

"No, thank you. Just wanted to see you," Duke said.

A tall man on a white horse stopped in front of them. Ellie looked up and recognized Soapy Smith.

"Miss Ellie Webster," Smith drawled as he tipped his hat.

"How do you do?" Ellie nodded politely.

"As you may know, all the businesses in the area contribute to my services," Smith began.

"She's with me." Duke stood and put his arm on her shoulder. "We've paid up," he added, squeezing her shoulder when Ellie opened her mouth to protest.

"Oh," Smith said as he looked from Duke to Ellie. "Well, all right. I'll check on that tomorrow. Evening." He tipped his hat and rode away.

Ellie stood up as Duke's arm dropped from her shoulder. "I am *not* with you," she said indignantly, "I can't have people thinking I'm not a lady. And if you think one dinner gives you the right—"

"Just trying to help," Duke said, palms up. "He wanted you to pay him a bribe, a graft."

"What?"

"I said you were with me so he'd leave you alone."

"You mean he—" Ellie started. "Smith wanted our business to give him money?"

"Yes. I was only trying to get him to go away."

She sat down again. "Oh. Um, thanks." She attempted to dismiss her anger at being mistaken for a loose woman and focus on the problem of Soapy Smith. Would he return to bother her?

"You're welcome." Duke sat next to her. "I thought something like this might happen. I'm sorry I took a little liberty there, but it was the first idea that came into my head."

"Oh. But I still don't want you telling people—" Her face blushed again. "I mean, I'm—" She wasn't sure how to finish the sentence without sounding ungrateful to him for trying to help her a moment ago.

"I understand. I apologize."

"Thank you. I'm sorry for my overreaction." Ellie nodded to where Soapy rode his horse down the street. "You know, you shouldn't encourage him by giving him money."

"The whole town gives him money. I'd be a fool not to."

"Really? How awful." She thought of Ada's comment the other day. That must have been what she was trying to ask about—if Soapy had her pay any graft yet.

"I'm afraid that things are not perfect here in Skagway, Ellie."

"I guess not," she said, wondering why the law hadn't rid the town of corruption. She'd read in the papers about this kind of thing happening in New York or Chicago, but a small town like Skagway should be easier to enforce.

"But I didn't come here to discuss local politics." Duke smiled and took her hand in his. "Ellie, would you give me the pleasure of another dinner?"

She hesitated. Could she afford to take a night off? That was a lot of money to turn down. But she wanted to see Duke again.

"Or tea, or whatever else you'd like to do," he pleaded.

"Business is slower in the morning." She stared into his pure blue eyes. "Maybe breakfast?"

"I would love to have breakfast with you." He beamed that dazzling smile of his. "Tomorrow?"

"No. I have to make some pies in advance. The next day?"

"Day after tomorrow. Thank you, Miss Ellie." Duke kissed her hand so softly she barely felt the pressure of his lips, the warmth of his breath. She shivered.

"Got enough wood now," Billy announced as he came around the corner.

Ellie and Duke both stood, and he dropped her hand.

"Oh, um, good," Ellie stammered, feeling as if she'd been caught stealing cookies from Mama's pantry.

A sheepish grin spread over Duke's face. "Okay, well, I'd better be going."

"Thanks for dinner the other day," Billy said.

Duke nodded. "You're welcome. I'll see you soon."

"Oh, all right," Billy replied.

"Good night, Duke," Ellie said as he started to turn away.

He stopped and looked back at her. "Good night, lovely lady." He winked at her, then walked away whistling.

"What is going on?" Billy asked Ellie.

Her blush returned. "Um, nothing. We're having breakfast with him day after tomorrow."

Billy chuckled. "Are you two getting sweet on each other?"

Ellie drew herself up to her full height. "I am eighteen years old, and I can have breakfast with Duke Masterson if I want to."

"But you want me to go as a chaperone."

"Of course. I am a lady." Her cheeks remained hot as she stuck her nose in the air and poured dehydrated apples into a pan with as much dignity as she could muster.

"Okay, I'll go with you. But do you know how red your cheeks are right now?"

Ellie threw an apple at him in response as she tried not to laugh.

Duke turned up at the tent the next morning, a parcel wrapped in brown paper tucked under his arm.

"Hey, Duke. Whatcha got?"

"Hello, Billy. Ellie. I have a little something here for Ellie. You see, I've been worried about her not having any firearm protection. You never know when it might come in handy."

Ellie couldn't believe he'd go to such lengths for her. "You bought me a gun?"

"And ammunition. You ever shot a gun before?"

"We grew up on a farm. Billy and I have hunted most of our lives."

Duke shrugged. "Guess I should've thought of that. But this little beauty might be new to you." He unwrapped the brown paper and pulled out a tiny handgun, with ivory grips and two silver barrels, one on top of the other, about three inches long.

"That a derringer?" Billy looked at the flat little pistol in Duke's palm.

"Yep. This .41 Remington can do more damage than you might expect. Let's walk out of town a little and have some target practice."

Ellie shook her head and folded her arms. "We'll have customers in about fifteen minutes."

"This won't take long and it's necessary. You're out of sorts with Soapy Smith and half the town has a crush on you."

Ellie sighed. "Oh, all right, if it will make you feel better." Maybe he was right.

They walked toward the forest, Duke and Billy collecting boxes of trash along the way. Duke stopped in front of a stump and placed an empty box of soap flakes on top of it, then surveyed the area carefully.

"We're out of people's way. Let's try it here." Duke stood about five feet from the stump, moved the latch on the derringer, and the barrel flipped up to reveal the end of the double barrels. He deftly removed two cartridges from the box and loaded the gun then put it back together.

"I'll try one first." He pulled the hammer back, worked the trigger, and a loud pop sounded. When the smoke cleared, the soapbox was intact.

"Can I try?" Billy asked.

"Use the sights," Ellie reminded him, wondering if Duke knew anything about guns.

Billy took the gun from Duke carefully, aimed, and knocked the soap box off the stump with a bang, causing a few flakes to flutter to the ground. "Boy, that was fun! Can I do it again?"

Duke grinned back at him. "Guess you know more about this than I do. Sure."

Billy replaced the soap box, placed an empty, hot-cereal box on another stump, reloaded, and shot both off. "Here, Ellie, you try it now." He put the boxes on the stumps for her.

Duke handed Ellie two cartridges. Because the mechanism was stiff, Ellie had to work the latch and the hammer deliberately. But she took her time to load and aim carefully, lining up the post on the barrel with the notch at the back. The gun barked and white smoke puffed out of the barrel, the bullet hitting the center of the box, which flew off the stump. She grinned at Billy, then turned to Duke in triumph.

"Great job, Ellie. Try another one," Duke encouraged her.

Ellie stepped back about seven feet from the stump. Her shot nicked the top of the other box. It fell over.

"It's really designed for close range. But you shoot well, Ellie."

"Thank you." Ellie shrugged. "I don't think I'm going to need this, but the gesture."

Duke bowed and swept his hat before her. "You are welcome, my lady. Anything to keep you safe."

THE TABLES AT the Burkhard House were set the same for breakfast as they were for dinner. As Duke pulled out a chair for her, Ellie admired the china and white table linens.

"Ellie, is that a new blouse? It's very pretty," Duke noted as he sat down.

"Yes, thank you," Ellie answered, pleased he noticed the blouse that Ada had lent her.

"And you're wearing your cameo necklace, too," he added.

"You are very observant."

Duke's blue eyes glittered. "I am where you're concerned."

"So, what's good for breakfast here?" asked Billy.

"Sourdough pancakes and French toast are our specialties," the waiter answered behind Billy's left shoulder.

"I'll have the pancakes," Ellie ordered, "and coffee, please."

"The same." Duke smiled at her.

"The French toast," Billy said, "and coffee, too."

Duke turned to him. "So Billy, how do you like Skagway?"

"It's nice enough. Beats living on the trail. Haven't had time off to see much yet. The pie business is kind of a two-person operation," he added.

"I'm sure you're very helpful to Ellie."

"Oh, yes. I couldn't bake the pies, serve the customers, and take the money all by myself," she agreed. "I need him to keep things going."

"And we're doing pretty good," Billy explained with the air of a seasoned businessman. "Keeping busy."

Duke nodded. "It will be nice to have a big nest egg for your mama."

"Yep," Billy said as the waiter poured coffee.

"And how do you like Skagway, Ellie?" Duke asked.

"Oh, same as Billy. It's a little different, but there are some nice people here." Her cheeks heated as she met his eyes.

"Yes, I've found that too." Duke's smile grew into a grin.

"Pancakes and French toast," the waiter announced as he served their plates and placed syrup on the table.

"So that's what French toast is," Billy murmured at the slices of bread on his plate.

"If it doesn't look good, I'll trade you," Duke offered.

"No, it's fine. Just wondered what it was." Billy poured syrup on his plate.

"So, Duke, what are your plans for the winter?" Ellie asked.

"Most people clear out of here in the winter, and I'm not fond of snow, so I'll head back to San Francisco," Duke explained as he cut up his pancakes. "I wish you could go with me," he added then bit his lip.

Ellie's eyes widened at his impertinence, then she replied as if he hadn't said the last sentence, "We'll be going back home, of course."

"Yes, I figured that. We should probably book our passage soon. May I help you get tickets?"

"Thank you. That would be nice. We'll be ready to go next month or early September."

"All right, I'll look into it," Duke replied.

"You know, this French toast is pretty good," Billy interjected. "You want a bite, Ellie?"

"Sure." She ate the piece he set on her plate.

"Hey, Billy, we ought to get you to San Francisco one day. They have more fancy food there than you'll find in a lifetime up here—French and Italian—more chefs from around the world than you can shake a stick at. And Ellie, they've got theaters, fine bookstores, department stores, and all the creature comforts you could think of. Gas lighting, telegraph service. More fine things than Red Cloud." He waved his fork. "I'm guessing, of course."

Ellie smiled at the picture Duke painted.

"And the weather is mild. It rains, but it doesn't snow in the wintertime. You won't have to trudge through the snow or bundle up against the cold. It's a beautiful city, too. Elegant buildings and cultured people." Duke smiled, staring off into space as if everything he'd described was right outside the door.

"Don't they have miners, too?" Billy asked.

Duke shrugged. "Some. But most of the forty-niners have left by now. A second generation has come in, more into business and trade. So the city has grown up a bit."

She smiled at the light in his eyes. "Sounds like you really like San Francisco."

"Yes, it's my favorite place in the world, with the exception of where you are." He winked at her.

She smiled back at him as their eyes met for a moment. She felt herself being drawn to him, this charming man she knew so little about, and wondered if she'd ever stop blushing in his presence.

THE FOURTH OF July was a big holiday in Skagway. Everyone stopped work to watch the parade. Billy stood next to his freckled friend, Harry. Seated between Duke and Dan, Ellie watched from one of the pie stand benches.

"We appreciate the invitation," Dan said to her.

"You're welcome. I figured since the parade was on our street, you might as well have a good place to watch it."

"Thanks, Ellie." Duke put his hand on her shoulder. She almost shrugged it off, but let it linger there. His warm strength was comforting.

As they watched, a band played *The Stars and Stripes Forever* and the girls from the saloons went by, decked in red, white, and blue bunting and little else.

"Great piece of music," Duke murmured.

"Yes, that Sousa sure can write them." Ellie was shocked at the brazenness of the women. Maybe they were making a lot of money, but there was a limit to what a proper girl would do. These women were certainly not decent. She was glad Duke wasn't staring at them like some other men were doing.

"Look who's grand marshal," Billy said as Soapy Smith rode by, looking tall and commanding on his white horse. As he went by, Ellie refused to look the man in the face, instead focusing on the horse.

She wondered if he'd come back to ask for money. How much would he want, and would they still have enough for the mortgage if they had to pay him a bribe?

"Happy Independence Day." Dan shook Ellie's and Billy's hands as the parade ended. "Better get back to business, but don't be strangers."

"Thanks, you too!" Ellie called as he started to walk away.

Duke winked at her. "People will be hungry and thirsty now. A good day for making money."

Ellie grabbed her apron and started to wait on the line of men already forming outside the tent. "Freshly made pie, fifty cents!" she called to the crowd on the street.

Ralph nodded as he took his pie from her. "Happy Fourth of July, Miss Ellie."

Jim echoed behind him, "Happy Fourth."

"Happy Fourth to you, too." She smiled at them, still thinking about the grin on Duke's face. He seemed so much like a little boy sometimes, with that twinkle in his eye. How could some men do that—have that little boy look to them, but still be all man at the same time?

"ANOTHER BEER, DUKE," a thin man shouted as he waved his glass in the air.

"Be right there, sir," Duke called down the bar as he set out a couple drinks for the miners at the other end.

Usually, Duke could keep his mind on his work and get the orders straight for his customers, but he was barely thinking about the men in front of him today. Ellie had let his arm stay around her shoulders yesterday. And she'd smiled at him so sincerely. She was starting to like him, he thought.

Duke poured a beer for the thin man then scanned the saloon to make sure everyone else was settled.

Before, Ellie appeared to enjoy his company. She'd often blushed when he was around, but it was hard to tell if she cared about him. Now, she agreed to carry the gun to make him feel better, although she obviously thought it wasn't necessary. Plus, Ellie had invited him—well, him and Dan—to watch the parade with them. And she let his hand stay on her shoulder, almost as if she wanted him to touch her.

The tide was turning. Soon Ellie would see his feelings for her and realize that she felt the same way, too. He was sure she would grow to love him at the rate they were going. If he could make it happen quickly enough, she would be going to San Francisco with him. As his bride.

"Hey, Duke, another round. Have you gone deaf?"

"Sorry, here you go."

How could he see her more often, with them both hard at work this summer? Absence might make the heart grow fonder, but he needed to be sure. He thought about his parents and how they'd been separated when his father was in the Cavalry. Then he remembered the letters he wrote to his mother, and how she'd cherished them for the rest of her life.

That was it! He would write a love letter to Ellie. She'd read it and know how much he loved her. He'd write one tonight.

"MISS ELLIE, THIS is for you," Ralph said as he handed her an envelope the next morning.

"Oh, thanks." Ellie set down the stove wood and looked at the envelope. The tidy handwriting said, "To Miss Ellie Webster," across the front. She sat down and slit open the envelope with the knife she'd use to cut pies later.

Dear Ellie,

Thank you for inviting us to watch the parade with you, and for indulging my wishes with the target practice and meals. You are a lovely young lady, and I enjoy your company.

When I say lovely, I mean you are endowed with a natural beauty that stands out in a crowded room. Your soft, wavy hair, your clear, sun-kissed skin would make any man proud to stand next to you. But more than that, your integrity and warmth sparkle through your eyes. Your compassion and principles drive you to honest, forthright actions, which I admire. You are all woman, Ellie, but also all that is good and right in this world. In contrast to the shady goings-on in this town, you shine as an example of what a good person should be.

I have enjoyed your company of late and hope to see more of you in the future, as time permits in your busy schedule. I would not want to do anything to keep you from the goal of saving your family's farm. But when you have a moment, I hope you think of me in a favorable light. I'd like to share any extra hours with you as you see fit. I take the liberty of being forward, to tell you that I spend much time thinking of you and hope to become closer to you, possibly as a suitor. I have only the best intentions and hope to tell you more of my plans one day in person.

Until then, please know that I think the world of you, and end this letter as your obedient servant.

Sincerely,
Duke

"Oh, my. Good thing I was sitting down." Ellie's heart beat fast as emotions filled her breast. She was flattered at how he admired her, saw all those good qualities in her character, and surprised by the depth of his feeling and his intent to be a suitor. Duke wanted to marry her? All this time, she thought he was just flirting with her, enjoying her company as a rare woman with morals in this town, but he really cared for her, maybe even loved her. That explained that impertinent comment at breakfast—it was a hint of his feelings. Was that why he was so insistent on protecting her from Soapy Smith? Because he loved her?

Ellie heard Billy add wood to the stove behind her, but didn't speak to him, only stared at the letter in her hands.

So Duke was courting her. He asked to spend time with her. What should she do? Spending more time with him would encourage him in his wooing. Did she want that? Her only purpose in being here was to make money and get back to Mama as soon as possible. She wasn't looking for any gentleman callers, certainly not to get married. But his tender words tugged at her heart. She had to admit she was growing fond of Duke. But was that enough to encourage his hopes? Should she put a stop to this now?

"What is that?" Billy asked behind her.

"Duke wrote me a letter." Her cheeks grew hot as she folded the letter, put it in her pocket, and went to wash the knife.

"Ah, a love letter?"

"Kind of. Is the stove hot enough?" Ellie asked quickly to get Billy back to work. She'd have to sort this out later. Their customers would be here soon, and she needed to put the next round of pies in the oven.

THREE DAYS WENT by without further contact with Duke. Ellie kept busy with the pie tent, but thought about him at odd moments throughout the day. Sometimes, while making pies, she recalled all the nice things he had said and done for her.

Duke listened and understood her the night they returned to Skagway. He'd helped her get settled and celebrated their first big day as a business, and he'd tried to negotiate with Soapy Smith, whom she still half-expected to show up demanding money from her again.

While she got apples ready for boiling, she remembered how he'd called her beautiful and "all that is good and right in this world." And he had a fondness for music and reading. With all that, how could she think badly of Duke?

Other times, when she served customers, she remembered his cavalier attitude and how he'd insulted her the first time they'd met. Duke was not perfect. But then, was anybody? Even her father had sunk them in a debt they couldn't pay, until Ellie and Billy came to the gold rush. It wasn't Papa's fault, really, but he wasn't as perfect as she'd thought when she was younger.

Most of the time, Ellie avoided the real question. What did she feel for Duke, and what should she do? She was fond of him, and thought of the times his touch made her warm and even shiver.

Did she love him? How could she fall in love with anyone, out here in the middle of nowhere, when her job was to make money, keep Billy safe, and return to Mama? Even if she did love him—which she wasn't saying she did—wasn't her obligation to her family, to going back to Nebraska to pay off the mortgage? According to the plan, there wasn't any room for thoughts of running off to San Francisco with some man. No, even if she did have feelings for Duke, she couldn't marry him.

Getting married to Duke would mean moving to San Francisco and becoming a bartender's wife. As a wife, she'd follow her husband, tending bar with him until children were born, and then she'd have to take care of them in an apartment. She'd heard city apartments were small, cramped things, not like the big farmhouses back home. That didn't sound like much of a life.

"Miss, could I have a fork?" a man asked as he took his plate of pie.

"Oh, sorry." Ellie gave him one. She was getting so absentminded lately. This thing with Duke was becoming ridiculous, especially when it got in the way of the pie tent. That was it. She had to break it off cleanly and tell him she was not interested, move on, and get her mind back on the business.

AFTER WORK, SOAPY Smith rode down the street and stopped at the tent. "Evening, Miss Ellie," he said as he tipped his broad-rimmed hat.

Ellie shot Billy a look and he ran to find Duke.

"Evening," she said as calmly as she could. She wouldn't let someone like Soapy get the best of her.

"So I've been checking my records, and Mr. Masterson has paid for the Frisco, but nothing more." His horse nickered.

"I'm sure there's just a mix up." As she remembered the derringer in her pocket, her stomach fluttered. She couldn't imagine drawing a weapon on anyone for the sake of money, even a scoundrel like Soapy Smith.

"That may be. In the meantime, I'll need an installment."

"You don't supply any services for me, Mr. Smith, so I'm hard-pressed to see why I should pay you anything."

"Oh, you'd be surprised how much security my men provide in this town." His tone suggested there would be less security for her if she didn't pay.

"Perhaps." She racked her brain for an answer. "As you know, Mr. Masterson and I are, ah, business partners in a way. How do I know you haven't already received money from him?"

He looked her up and down in a way that made her flesh crawl. "He has chosen a pretty partner, I must say. Perhaps we could come to some sort of arrangement, if you'd like to barter for it?"

"I am not that kind of woman, Mr. Smith," she said as evenly as she could.

"That would make it more interesting, don't you think, Miss Ellie?" His eyes lingered on her body.

She took a deep breath and raised her chin. "I am asking you to leave and not come back, until Mr. Masterson and I are both here to discuss payments with you."

"I'll not be put off forever. I usually get what I want in this town and in a timely manner."

"Goodbye." She turned away from him, and walked in the direction of the Frisco with her head high, making her steps look as confident as she could. But inside she was shaking.

Plowing through the crowd as if the street were empty, Duke strode toward her. She could see Billy behind him. Duke reached out and took her hands in his.

"Are you all right?"

She felt rattled, but his touch was soothing. "Um, I guess so."

"He asked for money?"

"And insinuated more." She took a sharp breath to keep the tears from her eyes.

"Oh, Ellie. I wish one of us had been there to—"

"I put him off. Told him I wouldn't speak to him without you present."

"Good job. That was the right thing to do."

Billy nodded. "But now what?"

"I'll handle him. I'll think of something," Duke said.

She let go of his hands. "Duke, I don't want you to give that man money to reward him."

"I know that, but if we do nothing he'll harass you again. Leave it to me. I'll take care of it."

Billy shook his hand with his left. "Thank you."

"You're welcome. Anything for you two." He flashed another of his dazzling smiles.

But Ellie wondered if it would be that simple. Trying to ignore the fear in her gut, she vowed to keep Billy close from now on.

"Ellie, about the letter—"

She couldn't deal with his wooing on top of everything else right now. "Duke, the letter was sweet, but could we save that for another time?"

"Of course," he said as she walked away from him.

CHAPTER SEVEN

ELLIE SAT NEXT to Duke on the church pew. How did she get talked into this? She'd been determined not to encourage his suit, and yet here she was listening to hymns with him on a Sunday afternoon.

The willowy young lady at the lectern sang with pure, high notes as she launched into the chorus of *Shall We Gather at the River*. Ellie always liked the song. She turned to Duke to tell him, but he wasn't looking her way. Duke gazed out the window at the thick trees, listening with a faraway look in his eyes and a slight smile on his lips, his right foot tapping slightly to the rhythm. Ellie softened at the dear expression on his face, and she wondered what he was thinking about. Was he remembering hymns from his past?

Going to church back home, she'd sat with her family and all their neighbors. She'd seen young women go from joyous brides her age to weary wives in the space of a few years. So many women were worn down from the burden of helping their husbands. She wouldn't get married and become one of them. Even if Duke was nice to her, that didn't guarantee it would be enough to keep her from that fate.

Ellie looked at the dark wood pews and the white walls of the Union Church. There were no stained glass windows or artwork on the walls, but there was no lack of emotion in the audience. The crowd around them clapped fervently then seemed transfixed as the songstress started *Bringing in the Sheaves*. All eyes locked on the lovely guest singer, brought in especially from Oregon for recitals across Alaska.

Everyone was dressed in their Sunday best, the townsmen in dressy clothes and the miners in the cleanest shirts and pants they had. Little Lizzie, seated next to Ellie, had her brightest, starchiest pinafore on over her nicest dress. Ellie smiled at Lizzie, and Robert next to her.

Ada was at the pie tent helping Billy while Ellie "enjoyed a little high culture." Ellie shook her head, still not sure what persuaded her to leave the business for the afternoon to accompany Duke here. But she had to admit, she was enjoying the music, until she thought about women and their fates in marriage. A fate she wanted to avoid.

The singer curtsied at the end of the song, and the crowd applauded boisterously. The singer first looked shocked at the whoops and hollers, but smiled at them. A couple men shouted, "Bravo!" Duke grinned at Ellie, as if enjoying a joke.

"Not the typical recital, I suppose," he said in her ear.

"No. We don't holler in church back home," Ellie replied as she clapped.

The audience rose to leave and Duke offered his arm to Ellie. She blinked as he led her out into the bright sunshine.

"Shall we take a stroll before we return to work?" Duke suggested as Lizzie and Robert joined them.

"No, thank you. I should get back to the pies."

"Oh, all right." They turned toward Broadway. "Did you enjoy the music?"

"Yes, I did, thank you. I haven't heard church hymns in so long. It reminded me of home." She'd leave it there. No need to distress him with her decision not to get married.

"Me, too." Duke stopped and opened his mouth, as if he was going to say something, then decided against it.

She started down the boardwalk, the children tagging along behind them. "I'm glad there was such a big audience."

"Yes, this town supports all kinds of events. It's good to see the families there, too."

She thought back to the tired wives she'd known. "Yes."

He steered her gently around a mud puddle as they crossed the street, then they stopped in front of the pie tent. "You haven't heard anymore from Soapy?"

Her heart beat faster as she recalled Soapy's eyes on her body. "No, I haven't. Thank you for a pleasant afternoon, Duke."

"All my pleasure," Duke answered as he took her hand from his arm and kissed it before releasing it, his warm breath sending a shiver down her spine.

"Talk to you later," Ellie called as she took the apron from a grinning Ada.

I shouldn't have gone with him, Ellie thought as she tied her apron strings. *Now I'll never find a way to let him down easy. I don't want to break his heart. But I guess I'll have to in the end.*

Ada tousled Robert's hair. "How was the concert?"

"Very nice, talented singer," Ellie replied as she opened the stove door to check on the pies.

Ada's dimples deepened. "And your escort?"

"Oh, fine. When did these pies go in?"

"They should be ready in about ten minutes. Did Duke enjoy the music, too?"

"I think so." Heat rose into her face. "Ada, just because I went to a recital with him doesn't mean I'm going to marry him."

Ada grinned. "I didn't say anything about marriage."

"No, but you were thinking it."

A pudgy young man came up to her, cap in hand. "Miss Ellie, would you like me to do anything back here for you?"

"Um, not right now, Tim. You can ask Billy if he needs something."

Before Ada and her children started across the street toward the hotel, she said, "Let's talk later, okay?"

"Yes. Thanks for the help. Billy, is everything all right?"

"Yep. Everything's under control," Billy called over his shoulder as he took money from a customer.

Under control. Was she keeping things with Duke under control? That was the question.

THE NEXT DAY, Ellie and Billy sold pie as fast as she could make it. "I have something for Miss Ellie," a man said over the murmurs of the men waiting in line.

"I'm over here," Ellie called as she rolled out pie dough on the back table. Ralph placed an envelope in her hand, and Ellie smiled politely at him. *Oh no, not another one.* She stuffed it in her apron pocket, determined to look at it later when she had time, and finished getting the next round of pies in the oven.

But she couldn't dismiss the letter from her head. For the next hour, as she made pies, or smiled absently at the men as they took their pie or washed dishes for her, her mind was on the unopened envelope in her pocket.

She was sure it was from Duke, even though she hadn't looked at the handwriting on the envelope. She'd never responded to the other letter, needing to think about it first, and then deciding not to encourage him. When Soapy Smith had come by she'd been too rattled to handle a wooing suitor at the same time. It was probably rude for her not to mention the letter at the recital. She should have turned him down by now.

What did he think about her silence? Was he still pursuing her? He appeared to be. Her heart pounded as she wondered what Duke wrote, and found herself hoping he had sweet things to say.

Silly girl, she told herself. *You simply like to be flattered. Don't be a fool. Mama raised you proper. Don't fall for the first man who's nice to you.*

All the same, her hands shook when she finally opened the envelope. She took a steadying breath and read.

Dear Ellie,

I fear that my first letter offended you. If so, I apologize. I have no desire to offend you in any way. I only wrote to let you know that I have sincere and good intentions toward you. Your cordial behavior at the recital gives me hope that my attentions are not all in vain.

Your lovely face is often in my mind and your voice in my ear as I go through my lonely days. I remember your silver laughter, the moral strength in your actions, and I feel so lucky to have had your company this summer. However things work out between us, I have been privileged to have your friendship, to know such a sweet and forthright lady. You truly are a gem, a jewel, in my life. I strive to be worthy of you.

I hope to be able to explain my feelings in person one day soon. I await your convenience. Your obedient servant always,

Duke

Ellie swallowed around the lump in her throat. Now he was begging for her answer. What could she say? *Duke, I love your flattery, but I don't want to marry you? I have feelings for you, but don't waste your time?* She had to be decisive and put an end to his pursuit. She couldn't string him along like a fish on a line. She'd write him a response tonight.

As she made and served pie, and directed Billy and the volunteers to do odd jobs, possible phrases wafted through her mind. *I enjoy your company, but I fear I don't have the same feelings. Your warmth and friendship have meant the world to me, but I can't marry you. Your intentions are quite flattering, but I don't plan to get married at this time.*

How did a young woman let someone down gently? She knew that girls did it all the time, but right now she couldn't think of the right combination of honesty and courtesy to turn him away.

"Something has to be done and soon!" the thin man in front of her shouted.

She dropped the fork in her hand. "I'm sorry, what?"

"About Soapy Smith and those thieves of his! We're holding a meeting tonight!"

Her gut squeezed as she remembered the way Soapy looked at her. Finally, something would be done about him.

The old man next in line said, "We're going to run them right out of town this time!"

"You bet we are," Sid agreed, straining the buttons on the waistcoat of his pinstripe suit.

"No. Let's get rid of them once and for all!" The thin man shook his fork at him. "String them up!"

"Let the law take—" Ellie started to say.

"He's got half the police force in his pocket. We can't rely on them. We'll solve this problem, you'll see." The thin man set his plate down and walked away.

"It's one thing to put them on the next ship out, but taking a life, that's different," the old man grumbled.

"Yes. Two wrongs don't make a right," Ellie agreed.

The old man promised, "I'll see if I can get them to listen to reason."

"Thank you, sir."

"You keep making these pies, honey," the old man said as he patted her hand.

She smiled at him, but bristled at his condescension. If only she were a man, she'd go to the meeting, too. Even though the customers treated her well, they didn't respect her like they would a man. To them, Ellie was the pie lady—brave for standing up to Soapy, but still just another pretty face, and they assumed that no brains came with it. It galled her sometimes.

She knew only one smooth talker in Skagway, but she'd never heard him speak in front of a group. She wondered if Duke could get these men to do the right thing, and hoped he'd try.

Duke. She sighed as she remembered the expression on his face during the recital, when he'd been enraptured by the music. He loved her and maybe she loved him, but she wouldn't marry him, and she couldn't keep him in limbo like this. She'd answer his letters tonight.

A FEW HOURS later, as Ellie and Billy were washing the last of the dishes, Duke stopped in front of their tent.

He tipped his derby. "Good evening, Miss Ellie. Billy."

"Hey, Duke."

"Hello," Ellie said as evenly as she could, cheeks burning at seeing the man she'd thought about all day.

Duke nodded at Ellie. "I'm on my way to a meeting, but I'd like to stop back afterward, if that's all right."

"Sure," Billy said. "Is this the one about Soapy Smith?"

"Yes. We hope to find a solution to that problem tonight." Duke stood tall and looked directly at Ellie. "I'll let you know how it goes, then," he added as he sauntered away.

As emotions roiled through her, Ellie twisted her apron in her hands. Maybe Duke could put an end to Soapy Smith's rule. And she'd have to refuse him gently, in person, somehow.

"What's got into you?" Billy asked.

Ellie told Billy about Duke's letters. "So now I'll have to talk to him and figure out a way to let him down easy."

"Are you sure you're not in love with him?"

"What?"

"I've seen the way you two look at each other."

"But—that's—" Ellie spluttered.

"If you want to marry him, I can take the money back home by myself." As the words left his mouth, screams and gunshots boomed down the street. Ellie picked up her skirts and ran as they continued firing.

Duke! Oh, God, don't let it be Duke. Don't let him be hurt.

It felt like hours to run the few blocks to the dock. Her breathing was ragged as she approached the crowd forming at the wharf. Blood rushing in her ears, her pulse racing, she pushed her way to the front to see what was happening.

Two men lay in pools of blood, guns beside them. Soapy Smith was dead. A man she didn't recognize was bleeding in the street, but still conscious, grimacing in pain. Another man knelt next to him, trying to staunch the blood oozing from his torso.

"Frank Reid went to stop him, and they drew almost at the same time," someone was explaining to the bystanders.

Ellie searched the faces in the crowd. She couldn't catch her breath, no matter how hard she tried, and plowed through the onlookers, toward the buildings, away from the crime. Where was Duke?

A pat on her shoulder made her turn around. Duke was looking down at her. Ellie wrapped her arms around him and buried her face in his chest as her eyes blurred with tears.

"Duke, you're all right."

"Ellie," he murmured as his strong arms held her. "Worried about me?"

"I heard the shots and I thought—" She let the sentence finish itself.

Duke gently lifted her face toward his. "It's all right. I'm okay," he said softly as he smiled at her and wiped a tear off her cheek with his thumb.

She took a shuddering breath. "I'm sorry to act like such an idiot."

"No, no. I'm touched," he answered. "Now, let's get out of here." He placed her arm on his and guided her to the boardwalk. The doctor ran by with his black bag, and men were shouting as they hurried to tell others what had happened.

Ellie's legs trembled beneath her but held her weight. "Wasn't thinking. I just reacted to the shots."

Duke beamed at her. "You didn't think, you just felt. I'd say that's good for you."

"What is that supposed to mean?"

He patted her hand. "Now, don't get all worked up. I meant, you can, ah, over think things once in a while. It's good for you to act on your feelings sometimes."

As Ellie's heartbeat slowed to normal, they walked in silence. The other people on the street were still a blur as she tried to collect her thoughts.

"So you do have feelings for me," Duke stated quietly.

"I do, but not what you think," Ellie replied slowly, choosing her words carefully.

"Well, I don't know who else you'd tear down the street for, except Billy. What would you call it?"

Ellie stopped and turned to face Duke, trying to ignore the twinkle in his eye. "Now, I'm serious here. I-I am fond of you. But I don't plan to marry you."

Duke's smile washed from his face and the twinkle disappeared.

"I want to be honest with you, Duke, and not mislead you."

"Well, Ellie," he said slowly, brows knitting together. "I appreciate that. But why wouldn't you marry me?"

"You are kind to me, and you say beautiful things, and your letters are very flattering." Ellie was looking at his chest now, finding it easier not to look into his eyes. "And that feels…nice. But I don't know if that's love. I don't think that's enough for me to give up my independence. And marrying you would mean a whole different life for me."

"It wouldn't have to." Duke drew her face toward his for the second time that day. "I wouldn't make you change your life."

She shook her head. "You wouldn't mean to. But I've seen lots of people get married, and the wife always ends up being the helpmate and servant. His ideas always come first. It was Papa's idea to take out that loan. Mama didn't want to do it."

"You and I are not like other people. Have I ever asked you to give up your plans?"

"No, but we're not married." She stopped herself before the word *yet* slipped out.

"Ellie Webster, I love you more than life itself, and I wouldn't treat you any different when we're married than I do today. You'll make your own decisions then, the same way you do now."

She looked at him dumbly. Duke swept her up in his arms and bent down, his lips touching hers. She opened her mouth slightly in surprise and their lips melded together, his moving slowly, tenderly on hers. As sensations swirled through her, her pulse raced and his warmth enveloped her.

Then his lips left hers and the moment passed. Duke's blue eyes sparkled like sapphires and he gently let go of her, keeping one arm around her waist.

"Think about it?" he asked softly.

"I don't know," she answered honestly. She didn't know what she was thinking now. Were the feelings she had for him love, or just confused vibrations lingering from the kiss? She felt as if the breath had been knocked out of her.

"There you are!" Billy called. They looked up to see him running toward them.

"Hey, Billy," Duke said. "You hear what happened?"

"To Soapy? Yep. I was wondering about Ellie."

"Oh, she was, ah, checking on me."

"I'm all right," Ellie said, trying to put on a bright smile to reassure her brother, but the smile felt weak. So much had happened in such a short time, she was almost faint. And she did not faint as a rule.

Duke guided her down the boardwalk with his arm still about her waist. "Here, let's get you back to your tent."

"So, did you see it happen?" Billy asked Duke.

"No. I was inside attending the meeting. We heard the shots and ran out like everybody else. By the time I got there, Soapy was dead and Frank Reid was lying on the ground. I guess Soapy tried to crash the meeting and Frank aimed to stop him by force."

"Frank's still alive?"

"Yep, but he's pretty well shot up. We'll see what happens." Duke guided Ellie to the bench in front of the tent and helped her sit down. "Your sister has had a shock. Do you have some water?"

"Sure. Let me get a cup," Billy said as he retrieved an enamel mug and filled it with water from the bucket. "Here, Ellie."

"Thanks." She accepted it, her hands shaking, and took a sip.

"Perfectly natural reaction to seeing those men lying there," Duke said. "Just take a breath."

That's not all I'm reacting to, Ellie thought. Her mind replayed the kiss, how her body melted when their lips met. *Was that love?* She stared at the cup.

"Maybe I should go. Let you get some rest," Duke said. "I'll leave you to your brother."

"Thank you." Billy shook his hand. "See you later."

"Good night, Ellie," Duke murmured as he kissed her hand tenderly.

"Good night, Duke," she whispered in reply.

They watched him go for a moment.

Billy coughed. "You want to tell me anything?"

"Oh, I ran down there like a fool, but Duke was okay." Her eyes started to tear up again. "Then he said I loved him, and he asked me to marry him. I said no, because I want to be independent," she concluded as she wiped the tears from her cheek.

"What did he say to that?"

"That I would still be independent if I wanted, and then he kissed me. And then you came." She sipped her water again.

"How did it feel?"

"What?"

"When he kissed you, how did it feel? Did it feel like that time Jimmy Anderson kissed you?"

Her eyes grew wide. "You knew about Jimmy Anderson?"

"Sure. I saw you in the barn. Did it feel like that?"

"No, different," she admitted.

"Better?"

Ellie's cheeks turned hot. Gosh, it seemed like she never blushed before, and now she couldn't stop since she'd met Duke. She nodded yes.

"I think you love him," Billy pronounced. "And I *know* he loves you."

"Now my seventeen-year-old brother is an expert in love?" Ellie regretted her sharp tone when she saw his crestfallen face. She touched his shoulder gently. "I'm sorry, Billy. I shouldn't have said that, but I don't know if I'm in love and right now I'm all mixed up with what's happened."

"It's okay." His face brightened. "Guess you've been through a lot in one day, seeing two men bleeding on the street, then getting kissed and proposed to. Why don't you sleep on it and we can talk later, if you want."

"Thanks, Billy. You're a good brother, you know that?"

He nodded. "You're a pretty good sister, too."

Ellie tossed and turned that night. Soapy Smith was dead, so that was one problem solved. But Ellie's feelings for Duke were deeper than she'd thought. Was she correct in turning down his proposal? If it was the right thing, why did it hurt so much?

Duke couldn't believe she'd refused him. She obviously loved him—ran all the way down the street after him when she thought he was in danger. And he'd never felt a kiss like that before. He knew it was more than lust that ran between them. But she'd turned down his proposal, wouldn't even commit to reconsidering.

He kicked a rock on the boardwalk back into the street as his gut twisted. It made no sense. He loved her and she loved him. What more could she want? Did she really think he'd run roughshod over her, after all the times he'd done nice things for her?

Maybe kissing her right after she'd seen a dead man was too much. But surely she'd forgive him for that mistake.

He turned onto a side street to get away from the crowd. At the beginning of the summer, his only goal was financial independence. But in the last few weeks, he'd wanted Ellie more than anything he'd ever wanted in the world. And now he'd lost her, for no logical reason.

There had to be a way to get her back. He needed a plan, something to make her realize how much she loved him and needed him in her life.

The next morning, as she loaded more wood in the stove, Ellie tried to make sense of what happened yesterday. She'd run blindly toward the gunshots, afraid that Duke was hurt or dead. She'd been afraid to lose him. So she did have feelings for him. Strong feelings. And he'd said he loved her. When he kissed her, well, she'd never experienced anything like that before.

But was that love or just one body calling to another? And what about marriage? Duke wouldn't try to change her, but he was a man, and men were self-centered. Could she believe him when he said she could be independent? She slammed the stove door shut.

Ellie had been of marriageable age for years, but she hadn't found anyone who made her consider the issue seriously. Mama was eighteen when she married Papa, but she'd wanted to be a farmer's wife.

Duke wanted Ellie to marry him, but he planned to bartend in San Francisco—not a life she wanted for herself. How much would he change for her? Ellie rolled out the piecrust dough furiously.

Billy stood at her elbow. "Feeling all right this morning?"

"Yes. Thanks."

"Want to talk about it?"

"No."

"Okay." He went about his chores.

"Knock, knock," Dan Palmer said as he tapped on the tent's entrance flap.

Ellie smiled at him. "Come in."

He stepped inside and held his hand out, then saw hers was covered in flour. "Maybe we shouldn't shake hands. Good morning."

"Hey, Dan," Billy called behind him as he entered the tent with a bucket of water.

"I came to check on Ellie. You all right?"

"Yes. I'm fine."

"Duke wanted to come, but he wasn't sure how you'd feel about that." Dan raised an eyebrow as Ellie's cheeks flushed. "So he sent me as his ambassador."

Ellie appreciated Duke's sensitivity. "Tell him I'm all right. Thank you."

"Want some pie?" Billy asked. "We'll have some ready in about half an hour."

Dan shook his head. "Not this time. You do have the best pie in town, but I should be going. Unless there's something I can do for you?"

"No, but we appreciate the offer."

"Tell Duke we said, 'hello'," Billy called as he turned to go. Dan missed the cutting look Ellie gave her brother in response.

"What are you doing?" Ellie hissed at him.

"Nothing," Billy answered nonchalantly. "Just trying to be nice to people. So you decided you don't want to marry him after all?"

"No. I don't want to be married. Now let's get back to work."

Billy sighed and set the bucket next to the stove.

Ellie shook her head in exasperation. "If you like him so much, *you* marry him."

"He's not in love with me, stupid."

"Oh, forget it." She placed the dough in a pie pan.

"All right, sis. Ruin your life, if you want to."

It was the worst thing he'd ever said to her. And she didn't have a retort for him.

THROUGHOUT THE DAY, Ellie attempted to block out thoughts of Duke and what had happened after Soapy Smith died. She threw herself into her work, getting pies out faster than usual, but scenes kept flashing in her head at odd times.

She sprinkled cinnamon and felt herself running down the street. She stoked the fire and saw Duke looking down at her. She gave a slice of pie to a customer and it was Duke's smile instead of his. She added water to the pan of dehydrated apples, and felt Duke's kiss. Blood rushed to her face in response.

This is ridiculous, she told herself. *Get a hold of yourself. So maybe I do love Duke, but I don't want to marry him. I didn't come all this way and survive the Chilkoot Trail just to be somebody's wife and helper. I am not going to leave Nebraska to be a bartender's wife in California. My job is to take Billy safely home where we both belong. Then I'll make a life for myself down there. We're going to close up shop in a few weeks and go back home with our money. That's the end of it. I'll never see Duke again.*

Tears stung her eyes as she thought of losing Duke forever. But she knew that's what her decision meant. They'd see each other a few more times in Skagway, and then they would go their separate ways. If that was the price she paid for choosing her own path in life, so be it.

"SHE SEEMED LIKE her usual self," Dan said to Duke as they straightened the furniture in the saloon.

"Well, I guess that's good." He wasn't sure if it was, though.

"She said to tell you she's all right."

"Yep, you told me already." Duke added a little wood to the fire. The air was cool that morning.

"I know, just reminding you."

So she still didn't want to marry him. That's why her message was so short. He wiped some clean glasses on the bar. He knew Ellie loved him. She'd proved it yesterday when her fear sent her racing to find him after the shootout. Why wouldn't she say yes, now that he told her she didn't have to give up her independence? Why wasn't that enough for her?

He couldn't just let her go. He'd have to think of a way to change her mind. The letters and the kiss were good, but he'd have to come up with something else, quick. Time was marching on, and they'd need to buy ship tickets for Seattle before long.

"Dan, you okay here by yourself for a little while during the mornings?"

"Sure."

"I'm going to pay a call tomorrow morning."

Ellie was stoking wood into the greedy stove the next day when she heard a familiar voice.

"Good morning, Ellie."

She looked up to see Duke tipping his hat, smiling down at her, and she stood up, trying to think of what to say that would be polite, but put him off.

"Glad to see you looking so well. I came to apologize for my behavior the other day."

She opened her mouth, but couldn't think of what to say.

"I shouldn't have kissed you then. I wanted to, but it was unchivalrous of me to take advantage of you at such a delicate moment."

"Um, thanks for the apology," she murmured, cheeks burning at his admission.

Billy returned from the outhouse as Duke was saying, "You're welcome. In penance, I'd like to work for you this morning. What can I do?"

"How about—" She looked around the tent. "Chopping some wood?"

"I'd be glad to." Duke waved his hand in a bow. "Your ax, my lady?"

"Over there." She pointed toward the back where the woodpile stood.

"I'll get right to it." Duke picked up the ax, tipped his hat, and walked to the forest at the end of the street.

"What's he doing chores for?" Billy asked Ellie.

"Kissing me in an unchivalrous way."

"Oh. While he's using my ax, what do you want me to do?"

She took off her apron. "You watch the stove and I'll go get some more water." She grabbed the bucket and walked away.

DUKE CHOPPED DOWN a small sapling and cut it into logs, wondering what Ellie thought of his appearance this morning. She looked a little confused. Not mad at him, but she didn't look thrilled to see him either. Maybe the apology was a good place to start. He'd see what she said when he got back with the wood.

When he returned to the tent, Ellie was nowhere in sight. Duke dumped the logs by the stove and started to stack them neatly.

Billy stood next to him and said quietly, "I think she loves you."

Duke looked up at him. "I think so, too."

"She doesn't want to get married. That's the problem." Billy ran his hand through his brown mop of hair. "I don't really know why."

"Thanks," Duke said as Ellie approached the tent, then went back to finishing his stack. So she did love him. It was marriage that was the issue. At least they had narrowed down the problem.

ELLIE SET THE water down and put her apron on. "Thanks for the wood."

"You're welcome. What else can I do?"

Ellie sighed. He was gallant wanting to help, but she didn't want to have to come up with jobs for him all morning. It was hard enough to keep her customers happy, and now she had him looking at her with bright eyes, waiting to obey her every word. How could she tell him to go away? "Duke, this is sweet, but—isn't it time for you to get the saloon ready for the day?"

"We don't open until noon and everything's set. What else can I do?"

Billy broke in, "The tent's getting a little saggy. Tighten the ropes?"

"Sure." Duke smiled and went outside.

She'd send him away when he was done with that chore. Ellie mixed piecrust dough and started to roll it out while Billy arranged the benches for customers.

Duke's voice came from the other side of the canvas. "So Ellie, business still good?"

"Yes. Staying pretty busy."

"What do you like about the pie business?"

"Oh, I guess the customers. They seem to appreciate the pie." She placed the apples in the crust.

"I can see why. It's delicious. And it probably reminds them of home and better days."

She nodded before she remembered he couldn't see her. "Yes, it probably does."

"Would you like to have your own restaurant some day?"

"That might be fun. But no pie on the menu, I'm getting pretty tired of making them." She put the next batch in the stove.

He chuckled. A puddle of water from a dip in the tent roof slid off and made a splat on the ground as the canvas straightened over her head.

Duke cleared his throat. "There are some married ladies with their own restaurants. One doesn't exclude the other."

Ellie's heart leaped at this. Could she have both? She wanted time to think about that before she answered him.

He didn't wait for her reply. "I checked ship schedules. The earliest we could get tickets for is the first week of August. Or we could wait a little while after that."

He was pushing her again. Ellie tried to think of something to say to let him down gently.

Billy shrugged. "I don't know, late August?"

Ellie didn't want to have to avoid Duke for so long before they left. "I'm getting tired of living in this tent. Let's try mid-August?"

"Yes, ma'am. I'll check the dates," Duke said as he appeared in the doorway again. "Tent better?"

"Yes, thank you." Ellie looked at the canvas stretched tight across the top.

"Anything for you, Ellie. Anything," he added as he came through the tent opening. His smile warmed her heart, but she said nothing in reply. "Any other chores I can do?"

"No, thank you."

"See you tomorrow then, lovely lady."

He didn't try to kiss her hand this time. Maybe he thought she'd had enough kissing lately, or that she might not let him this time.

She forgot to tell him she wasn't going to marry him until he'd already left.

CHAPTER EIGHT

ELLIE HELD THE scratchy wool yarn in her hands as Ada rolled it into a ball.

"Your hands are less red today. Is the cream helping?"

"Yes. They're much better." She noticed Ada always looked chipper, less worn out than the wives she knew back home. Maybe it was the town life that made a difference.

"Thanks for helping me with the yarn. I'd try to get the kids or Tom to do this, but the little ones are too squirrelly, and you know how men are. Speaking of men, how is Duke?"

The heat flooded her cheeks again and she wished it would go away. "He is well."

"And how are things between you?" Ada persisted.

Ellie shook her head. "I don't know. I guess I don't want to talk about it."

"Why? He's sweet on you, and I think you are on him, too."

"Ada, I am up here to keep Billy safe and make money for the farm. I'm not looking for romance."

Ada grinned. "It's not a bad thing if romance finds you, is it? Love is nothing to be afraid of, Ellie."

Ellie sighed and shook her head again. Her feelings and thoughts were too jumbled to share.

"All right, I will change subjects. I went to the women's suffrage meeting last week. We got a committee together to write a petition. Maybe you can sign it when it's ready?"

"Sure, I'd be happy to."

"I used that cheaper brand of baking powder when I made biscuits. Seems to work just fine. You might try it next time you need some. Have you been in Buxton's general store lately?"

"No. I usually send Billy on errands."

"How nice of you to get him out of the house once in a while. They got some fabric in last week. Some pretty calico I was looking at for Lizzie. She is growing so quickly, I think she'll need a new dress soon."

Ellie smiled as Ada rattled on about domestic things. It would be fun to have her own family, her own household to run some day, if it didn't mean giving up her independence. And maybe she could have her own restaurant. Could Duke be a part of that?

"Or do you think the blue would look better?" Ada asked.

"Sorry, the blue or…"

"Did I lose you for a minute there? I'm trying to choose between the blue or the green ribbon for Lizzie's dress."

"Oh, she looks so nice in blue."

Ada nodded. "That's what I was thinking. I'll have to get some more thread when I pick up the fabric, but I have everything else I need to get started. Maybe I'll do that tomorrow."

"Sounds fine to me." Ellie gave Ada the last little bit of yarn to wind on the ball.

"And there we are!" Ada beamed. "Thanks for your help."

"Anytime." Ellie stood. "I better get back."

Ada hugged her. "Don't be a stranger now. And if you do want to talk, I'm always here."

"Thanks, Ada." It was nice to have a good friend in town. If she ever did want to talk about Duke, she knew Ada would listen. But she wanted to sort things out in her own mind first.

Walking back to her tent—her boots kicking up the dust—Ellie thought of Duke's hand on her chin, the way his mouth met hers when they'd kissed, and her lips tingled. There were certainly something there, but was it enough? Could she be married and make her own decisions in life?

"STILL THE BEST pie in Alaska." Ralph tipped his dusty bowler as he handed in his plate.

Ellie laughed. "You say that every time."

"But it's true every time."

"True every time," Jim echoed behind him.

"Well, thank you," Ellie replied. She set the plate down and tossed another log in the wood stove.

"Sis, is it okay if I go fishing with Harry tonight?" Billy asked.

"Sure," Ellie answered as she imagined fresh salmon for dinner instead of beans and bacon.

"I'll help you clean up first."

"That's all right, I can do it by myself this time." Billy was so careful about his responsibilities. It would do him good to get out of the tent and go fishing with his friend.

DUKE SLUNG HIS coat over his shoulder. "I'll find Johnson and ask him about that shipment of whiskey."

"Good idea. Should be here by now," Dan replied.

Duke walked down the boardwalk toward the Long Branch Saloon. Johnson was usually at his station behind the bar by this time, and Duke would ask him why their share of the shipment was taking so long to reach them.

He entered the crowded barroom. Johnson wasn't at his post. Duke glanced around and noticed a familiar face he didn't expect to see there. Billy Webster was sitting at a table near the roulette wheel.

"What do you think you're doing here?" Duke barked. Billy jumped about a foot off his seat.

"Well, I was going fishing with Harry here." He indicated the plump, freckled young man on his right. "But the fishing wasn't very good…" His voice trailed off as his face grew red.

"Does your sister know you're here?" Duke raised an eyebrow as he wondered how to handle the situation.

"Oh, don't tell Ellie. I only had a beer," Billy pleaded.

Duke glanced at the table and noted the single glass in front of Billy's place.

"Only one?"

"Well, maybe two." Billy's cheeks turned a brighter shade of red.

"And you?" Duke turned on Harry in time to see his freckled face flush before he cast his gaze to the ground.

"Maybe three beers," he mumbled.

"And your folks?"

"No, my Pa doesn't know I'm here either."

"Pay your bill, and then I'm taking you out of here," Duke grumbled. He looked up to see Johnson at the bar. "Johnson, where's our whiskey?"

"Hey, Duke." Johnson, a fat man whose face was constantly flushed, smiled and gestured with his palms up. "Good to see you. I was just about to send that whiskey order over to your saloon."

"Better count those bottles first," Duke growled as he watched the boys pay the bartender.

"I'll make sure you get the right amount," Johnson said, then glanced at the boys at the bar. "Oh, are they related to you? On the house then."

"No. I think they better pay for that. Thanks."

Duke grabbed each of them by the elbow and marched them out into the dusty street. "You boys are too young for drinking. And I know your sister wouldn't approve," he added as he tugged on Billy's arm. "Doubt your folks would either," he said to Harry. "So I better take you home."

"Do you have ta?" Harry pleaded.

"Yes, I have ta. So where do you live?"

"At the packing company." He jerked a stubby finger, pointing up the road.

Still holding on to them, Duke marched them deliberately toward the pass. A small trail of dust followed behind and men stared, but let them go by without commenting.

"You know, if you were my kin, I'd come up with a pretty good punishment for your poor judgment. But since you're no kin of mine"—*yet*, he thought to himself in Billy's case—"I'll leave you to your elders. Harry, you staying with your pa?"

"Yep," he mumbled.

"I bet he'll know what to do with you then."

They marched up the street in silence, Duke wondering how severe he should be with Billy. Most boys try a little beer or whiskey at some time, but it was still a bad idea to encourage them. Duke was the closest thing to an older brother that Billy had in Alaska, so he felt somewhat responsible for his welfare. He thought about what his father would have done in the same situation.

"Billy, I'll offer to help Ellie if she wants somebody to give you a whipping." Duke glanced at Billy, an astonished look on his face. "Don't believe me?" Duke grumbled.

"No, I believe you. I just didn't expect it."

"Because I run a saloon myself?"

Billy nodded.

"I run a respectable bar, and we don't serve anyone too young to handle their drink. Alcohol is a comfort to a man, if he drinks responsibly, but a vice to one who drinks too young or too often. Remember that."

"Yes, sir," the boys answered in unison.

They drew up in front of the log building of Smith's Packers. Several men stood outside enjoying the evening sunshine. A man in scruffy overalls and a battered bowler hat stepped up to Duke and his charges.

"I'm his pa," he said, jerking a thumb at Harry. "He givin' you some trouble?"

Duke released Harry's elbow. "I found these two in the Long Branch, drinking beer. Thought you'd want to know."

The man took off his hat and thwacked it across Harry's head as the men laughed. "You idiot, what do you think you're doing? Where's the fishing poles?"

"At the crick," Harry mumbled.

"Well let's go get 'em, and then I'll deal with this," he said gruffly. He looked up at Duke and nodded curtly. "Thanks for bringing him home."

"You're welcome." Duke steered Billy around and started toward the pie tent.

They walked in silence on the boardwalk for a few moments, Billy lagging behind as much as he could within Duke's grasp.

"Want to explain what was going through your brain?"

Billy shrugged. "Celebrating getting my stitches out and my finger healing." He glanced at Duke. "All right, I'm tired of Ellie ordering me around. Why can't I make my own decisions for a change?"

"Your sister's just trying to keep you safe and make some money for your mama." She'd done a remarkable job so far. This was the first sign of rebellion from Billy he'd seen. And he hoped it would be the last.

"Do you have to tell Ellie?"

"She'd never forgive me if I didn't."

"Yep," Billy agreed resignedly.

ELLIE SAW THEM about a block away and waited, arms crossed and chin up, until they got close enough to speak. "What's this?"

Duke released Billy's elbow and pushed him toward her. "Caught him and his friend, Harry, in the Long Branch Saloon."

Ellie felt the familiar lead in the pit of her stomach—more evidence of her not keeping him safe while they were away from home. She wagged her finger under Billy's nose. "What were you doing in a saloon?"

"Drinkin' beer," Billy mumbled as he looked at his shoes.

"Mama and Papa raised you to be a proper young man, and here you are drinking when you're supposed to be fishing for tomorrow's dinner. What are we going to do with you?"

"Duke offered to whip me for you," Billy said, still focused on his shoes.

Ellie thought that's what Papa would have done. But it was absurd now. Billy was almost a man. She frowned at her brother. "I've half a mind to say yes to that offer. Up until now, you were acting like a responsible young man, helping with the business and all, but now you show poor judgment by drinking in one of the lowest saloons in this town. You're too young to drink, and you could have had your pockets picked, or worse. What do you have to say for yourself?"

Billy's face wore a pained expression. "I'm sorry, I was being stupid."

"And how are you going to make up for this, so Duke and I can be proud of you again?" She didn't have an answer to that herself, but it was worth asking the rhetorical question.

Billy thought for a moment. "I'll work double shifts. One for you and one for Duke."

Ellie almost smiled to herself at Billy's solution to her dilemma. It seemed like a fitting punishment for the crime, and wouldn't cost her any heartache. She looked at Duke's face and saw his lips were curling up. She put on a severe expression for Billy's benefit.

"Duke, is that all right with you?"

His face became stern. "Yep. I'd say two days would be enough."

Billy's expression eased a little.

"All right." Ellie shook her finger at him again. "Billy, you start tonight and then serve one more day with Duke. While you're there, do whatever he or Dan asks you to do."

"Yes, ma'am."

"Well, go to it." Ellie dismissed them with a wave of her hand.

Duke and Billy started toward the Frisco.

"Oh, Duke?" Ellie called.

He turned on his heel. "Yes, Ellie?"

"Thanks for bringing him home."

Duke's face brightened with a dazzling smile. "You're welcome. Have a lovely evening."

Hands on hips, Ellie sighed, and watched as they walked down the street—the two men she loved most in the world.

Did she just think that? She sighed again as she shook her head. It was true. The hard part was deciding what to do about it. Duke had proved again how caring and responsible he was, bringing Billy back here and helping with his punishment. He was a good man. But could she marry him?

When she was a girl, Ellie asked her grandma and mama once, "How do you know when he's the one?"

Grandma just said, "You'll know." Mama had nodded in agreement. Was it really that simple?

Life was proving to be more complicated than she expected. There were so many options, so many choices. Not all of them presented themselves as easily as when Billy came up with the terms of his own punishment. She'd have to think about it. And it looked like she'd have some quiet time by herself tonight to do that very thing. It would be nice to have some time to herself. It happened so rarely nowadays.

Ellie threaded a needle and picked up Billy's shirt to mend. It was still daylight this late in mid-July. She tied a knot in the thread as a whiskered gentleman walked up to the opening of the tent. She recognized him from the newspaper office.

He tipped his hat and held out his hand. She pinned the needle to her skirt and shook his hand.

"Miss Ellie, I'm Francis Harrington, newspaper editor. You may remember stepping into my office earlier this summer?"

"Yes, I remember."

"I'd like to run a feature article on you. May I ask you some questions?"

"All right."

He took a pencil and pad of paper from his coat pocket. "So where are you from?"

"Nebraska, near Red Cloud. My folks are farmers. Last name's Webster."

"And you came up with your brother this summer?"

"Yes, we came after gold, like most people. But we ran into some bad luck in the rapids near Lake Bennett, and came back here to make money with the pies."

Harrington smiled as he wrote notes. "I've heard they're the best pies in Alaska."

"Thank you."

"Care to share your secret on how you make them so delicious?"

Ellie laughed, thinking it wouldn't do to encourage competition. "Let's just say, there's a taste of home in every slice."

"That's fair." He nodded in agreement as he wrote down her statement. "Can't expect you to give away any trade secrets. Now, the other reason you've become so well loved is your run-in with Soapy, er, Jeff Smith. Care to comment on that?"

She decided not to alienate any Soapy allies in town. "I was simply trying to help a customer who'd misplaced his poke."

"It takes courage to stand up to Soapy Smith," Harrington prodded.

"I only did what anybody would've done." She shrugged as he looked up from his pad of paper.

"Did Soapy give you any trouble after that?"

"He asked for money, but Duke Masterson brushed him off for me." She figured that was common knowledge by now.

Harrington's pencil paused for a moment. "You are two remarkable people." He took more notes, and then looked up. "Any other comments you'd like to add?"

"No. Except we appreciate our customers. " Ellie smiled as sweetly as she could.

Harrington finished his notes, stood, and put his pencil and pad away. "Well, it's good to see your modesty, a quality that is sorely lacking in this town. And thanks for your time."

"You're welcome." They shook hands again and she watched him leave. That article should add to her image as a ladylike businesswoman, and perhaps also help Duke's reputation. It might give both of them more business. Not that she could serve pie any faster than she did now, but it might help Duke's saloon.

As she picked up Billy's shirt again, she thought it was nice to do something for Duke for a change. He had done so much for her, starting from the moment they'd met, when he'd made sure she didn't fall overboard.

Ellie chuckled at the memory. She'd been so angry at his forwardness, so determined on being a lady. Only now did she realize that it didn't mean following rules about clothes and etiquette, but, rather, it took a certain attitude to be a lady or gentleman. She could be a lady even without nice clothes and four, solid walls around her. All she had to do was treat people well and maintain her bearings in this crazy world.

And Duke, he could be a gentleman whether he was laying hands on ladies to save them from falling, or serving whiskey to grubby miners. Life was a funny thing. She sighed, and noticed the shirt in her lap. Time to get back to the chores at hand, she thought, and try to decide what to do about Duke.

DUKE HANDED BILLY the broom. "First, sweep the floor without disturbing the customers."

"Yes, sir." Billy went right to work on the dusty, plank floor by the bar.

"What are you doing here, Billy?" Ralph asked.

"I got caught drinkin' beer," he answered. "This is my punishment, working for Duke for a while."

"Very appropriate, to see what drink can do to a man. Some of these drunks will serve a good lesson to you."

"A good lesson," Jim agreed.

Duke smiled as he wiped the bar and thought of several customers that could apply to.

Billy nodded and went on sweeping the floor, going carefully around men's legs.

"Hey, Joe." Ralph tapped the shoulder of the man next to him. "Billy, here, is working off his punishment for drinking."

"Drink is a bad thing." Joe poked Billy in the chest. "Don't end up like us. Spending too much money on nothin' good for you."

"Yes, sir." Billy went on with his sweeping.

"Hey, what are you doing?" A man objected as the broom bumped into his boot.

"Sorry, sir." Billy stepped to another area.

Duke watched the whole scene from the bar. It looked like Billy was in for a long night. Maybe this was the appropriate consequence for him—much better than a whipping. Duke would have done it, if he had to, but was glad that Ellie had turned him down. It would be hard to be brutal to someone he'd grown to care about. Handing him a broom was a lot easier.

It would be grueling work for Billy, staying on his feet for a whole shift after working an entire day at the pie tent. A few rude customers, in addition, would be enough to keep Billy out of bars for a while. He hoped.

Duke handed a mug of coffee to a customer. "Fred, you've been in here most of the day. Time to lay off the hard stuff."

"Oh, all right, Duke."

Dan nudged Duke's elbow. "How's the prisoner doing?"

Duke winked at him. "Okay, I think. Let's see how he holds up. Give him three or four hours before we let him go home."

"Fine with me, partner." Dan picked up another bottle of whiskey. "Make him pour coffee when the floor's swept."

"Good plan," Duke agreed.

A group of men in the corner started singing *O Sole Mio*. Duke poured whiskey and watched Billy apologize to another customer as he swept around a bench. Duke wondered what Ellie was doing now. Probably something feminine like sewing or washing her hair. He imagined her brown, wavy hair cascading over her shoulders.

His mind flashed back to the kiss, how her body melted into his, how sweet her lips tasted. His hand shook as he poured a drink.

Don't think about it, you'll make yourself crazy, he told himself. *She won't even say she'll marry you—at this rate you'll never see that hair down.* And he still had to tell her about Red Cloud. He sighed. How could he get her to accept his proposal?

"Hey, Duke, need a drink over here!" a short man called to him from where he sat near the wood stove.

"Comin' right up." Duke flashed a smile at him as he poured. Had to keep the customers happy and figure out how to get Ellie to say yes. It was definitely going to be a long night for him, too, not just for Billy.

"Reporting for morning duty," Duke called at the tent entrance.

Ellie had forgotten about Duke's penance for kissing her. "Oh, good morning, Duke." It occurred to her that Duke was doing Billy's chores and vice versa.

"What can I do for you today?"

"How about hauling some water?" She handed him the bucket.

"Your wish is my command." Duke bowed as gracefully as one could while holding a bucket.

She smiled as she watched him walk away. What might look silly with another grown man always looked charming with Duke.

Billy yawned then looked at her. "Change your mind about marrying him yet?"

She took the apples off the stove. "The way to change a woman's mind is not to pester her about it."

Duke returned and laid the bucket at her feet. "What next?"

"Our sign's crooked. Can you straighten it?"

"Yes, ma'am."

Ellie thought she saw Duke and Billy gesturing to each other while she worked on pie crust. They were probably talking about her, but she wasn't going to pursue it.

"Anything else, my lady?"

The fixed sign looked fine. "Good job. No, thank you."

"All right then. Maybe I can stay and talk with you next time." He kissed her hand and the now-familiar warmth crept up her arm.

"See you tomorrow."

"See you tonight, Duke," Billy called as he walked away.

The day passed quickly as Ellie and Billy worked making and selling pies as usual. Billy moved a little slower, but seemed to have survived his first night at the saloon in good shape.

Ellie put the last set of pies in the stove.

Billy yawned. "You know what I was thinking? It's been quieter since Soapy died."

"I think you're right, Billy. It's been more settled in town since then."

A man in a dilapidated hat nodded. "It better be. They rounded up his men, the ones who didn't slip out of town already."

"Good observation, Billy." Ellie smiled at the customer. "I believe my little brother gets smarter every day. Now, if we can just get that mop of hair to lay flat. Why can't you have cooperative hair like Duke's?" she teased.

Billy grinned. "Ah, now I get compared to Duke. You *are* sweet on him."

Ellie threw an apple at him in response. He ducked out of the way easily. But she had to agree with him—yes, she was sweet on Duke. The problem was, what to do? Before last night, she'd decided to tell him she wouldn't marry him. Now, she wasn't sure.

He did have all the qualities she'd want in a good husband. Yesterday, he'd been so good with Billy, and careful of her wishes. Even this morning he was quiet when he got the hint not to push her about the proposal. Maybe she did want to marry Duke one day. But would it turn out the way she hoped? Or would she lose the independence she now treasured so much?

"Good morning." Duke's voice sailed into the tent as Ellie and Billy were getting ready for the day.

"Good morning, Duke," Ellie smiled at his freshly shaved face as he tipped his hat.

He kissed her hand. "Looking lovely as usual. Hi, Billy."

"Hi, Duke. Seems like I just saw you in the saloon."

"Yes. Thanks for the help last night."

Billy yawned. "Just part of the agreement. Are you here to help again?"

"If there's something I can do for you all," Duke said gallantly.

"Well, someone cut a huge load of wood for us yesterday—" Ellie began.

"Who's cutting your wood, besides me?"

"Some of the customers ask to do things for her, on account of her being a lady and all."

Duke raised his eyebrows. "I remember that, but is someone in particular doing this chore?'

Ellie checked the apples. "Only a kid."

"Probably has a crush on her," Billy added.

"Don't underestimate a kid with a crush on you," Duke cautioned.

She thought the young man was harmless, but he was a little too intense for her comfort.

"Make sure you don't encourage him."

Ellie laughed. "Now you're sounding jealous. Don't you start fretting about it."

Duke rubbed his goatee. "Maybe I am a little. You're surrounded by men every day."

"Well, you have no reason to be. At any rate, I don't need any wood this morning."

"What else I can do?"

She scanned the tent. "I really can't think of anything."

"I'll get some water." Billy picked up the bucket.

"Oh, I can get that for you," Duke offered.

"No, you sit here and keep her company." Billy left.

"Thanks for helping with Billy."

"You're welcome. He's a good kid."

"I'd like to think so, but I'm not taking care of him very well," she admitted.

"No, you're doing better than most could in your situation." Duke sat on a bench and watched Ellie pinch the top and bottom crusts together. "You do that so quickly."

"After a few hundred pies, I ought to be quick."

"My mother made good pies, too." Duke settled back and stared at the ceiling of the tent. "I've been meaning to tell you, she was born and bred in Nebraska."

Ellie looked up from her pies. "You're joking!"

"As a matter of fact, I was raised in Red Cloud."

"Duke Masterson, why didn't you tell me?" Ellie stood with her hands on her hips, feeling her body tense. She felt like a fool, rattling on about Red Cloud all these weeks not knowing he was raised there.

Duke shrugged sheepishly. "I don't know. I guess, at first, I thought you'd be more impressed with a city person, and then I just didn't know how to say it."

"Well, what you said now worked all right." She shook her head. "I can't believe you waited so long to tell me."

Billy came back with a full bucket of water.

"Duke has informed me he was raised in Red Cloud," she told him.

"Really?" Billy grinned. "What a coincidence! That's the closest town to our farm!"

Ellie ignored her brother, heart pounding, and interjected, "Anything else you ought to tell me?"

[145]

"That's all that comes to mind." He turned from her glare to Billy. "My father owns the livery stable there. About four years ago, I got tired of the winters and moved to San Francisco."

"Where you promptly started a career as a bartender," Ellie finished for him.

Duke nodded. "That's pretty much the story."

"I wonder why we didn't recognize you," Billy said.

"I was a skinny kid back then, and didn't fill out until later. And I went by my full name."

"Your folks still in town?"

"My mother died a few years ago, God rest her soul, but my father and brothers are still there at the livery."

Billy shook his head disbelievingly. "I've probably seen them every time we went to town and didn't know it."

Ellie slammed the oven door and Duke looked up at her.

"I'm sorry, Ellie, I didn't mean to *lie* to you."

She scowled at him. "Every time I think I have you figured out, you throw something else at me."

"I apologize." He looked at his clasped hands. "Really."

Ellie shook her head. "I really don't know what to think about you sometimes."

Billy smirked. "He's like a man of mystery. Never gets boring,"

"You think he's so wonderful, why don't the *two of you* get married!" Ellie threw down the cloth she was using for a hot pad and stormed off down the street.

DUKE STOOD TO follow Ellie, but Billy touched his arm. "Better let her calm down first."

They watched the clouds of dust form behind her as her skirt skimmed the street.

Duke let out a low whistle. "I didn't know she'd get so mad about it."

"She hates people lying to her." Billy laid the plates and forks on the table.

"It wasn't exactly a lie." He sighed. "Well, I guess my visit is over for the day. Tell her I apologize again, and hope she has a lovely day."

"Are you coming back?" Billy asked.

"Tomorrow, after she's simmered down."

"Good idea. Don't give up yet."

"Billy, you're a good friend and a good brother to her."

Billy grinned. "Thanks."

CHAPTER NINE

Ellie dashed down the street, blood rushing through her body like water in a rocky stream as she passed men walking and wagons rolling by. She swerved to avoid a large woman strolling ahead of her.

The nerve of that man! *He thinks he can sweet talk me, lie through his teeth if he wants to, and I'll let him get away with it! I am not one of his San Francisco girls that'll take anything from a handsome man. I have high moral standards.*

Ellie nodded to a pie customer. To think I even considered marrying that liar, she thought to herself. *Well, I'm glad I decided not to.* She marched down the street. *He'll be going back to San Francisco soon and good riddance to him. I hope I never see him again.*

She looked up and realized she was standing at the wharf. The last time she'd stood here, Soapy Smith was killed and Frank Reid died shortly after. And she'd been afraid for Duke. So much had happened since then.

She drew in a breath and looked out at the lush, green mountains leading into the sapphire-blue bay. Her shoulders relaxed as she looked at the puffs of white clouds skimming through the sunlit sky. A ship unloaded passengers and supplies at the dock, and a stream of people headed her way—another group of gold seekers or potential pie customers. She knew she should get back before Billy needed her at the tent.

Ellie sighed and started walking slowly back to town. Hopefully, Duke took the hint and left by now. She did not want to speak to him.

THAT AFTERNOON, MOST of the town's residents, and many of the miners passing through that day, attended Frank Reid's funeral. Long lines of men in black formed at the entrance to the cemetery and around the column at the gravesite.

Ellie and Billy stood quietly next to Duke and Dan, her anger set aside for the somber occasion. Ada and her husband were nearby. There was no business to conduct during the memorial service, and Ellie wanted to pay her respects to the man who had eliminated the problem of Soapy Smith.

A large, marble column marked Frank's grave. Several preachers said a few words, all wanting the honor of eulogizing the hero of Skagway.

"Frank Reid gave his life for this town, to make it safe for our families and the men who live and travel through here. We owe him gratitude and respect," Reverend Simpson said as a few parishioners sniffed into their handkerchiefs.

In her mind's eye, Ellie saw Frank Reid lying in a pool of blood near Soapy Smith's body. Her heart beat faster as she recalled the fear she'd felt that day, then looked at Duke on her right.

She sent up a silent *thank you* for Duke's safety, turned her thoughts back to the service, but then she remembered their kiss. This was not the time and place to dwell on her reaction to that kiss—this was a funeral.

The *thunk thunk* of rocks on wood brought her back to the present as men shoveled dirt onto the coffin. The crowd sang *Rock of Ages* and filed out past the grave. Ellie silently curtsied in front of the tall, white marker, taking a moment to read the inscription.

Frank Reid

He gave his life for the Honor of Skagway

Then she took Billy's arm and walked quickly back to their tent, avoiding Duke and Dan. She did not want to speak to Duke when she had such mixed emotions. One touch from him now might dispel the anger she felt toward his deception, and she wasn't sure she wanted to be done with it yet.

DUKE SHOWED UP at the tent the next morning, broad smile on his face as he tipped his hat and called, "Good morning!"

Ellie set the pie tins on the table. "I didn't think you'd come back so soon."

"Miss Ellie, I can't stay away from your charms." Duke grabbed and kissed her hand before she could stop him. "Anything I can do for you this morning?"

"No, thank you," she said curtly, trying to ignore the warmth that rushed into her kissed hand and face.

"So, how are things?" Duke responded as if he hadn't noticed the lack of welcome in her voice.

Billy returned from fetching water. "Hello, Duke."

"Good morning."

"We got some smoked salmon from a customer yesterday."

"Don't get that kind of thing back in Nebraska, do you?"

"No, we don't," Billy answered with a grin.

"I've been thinking. It's been a while since I've been home to see my folks. Maybe I'll go to Red Cloud for a visit after this summer."

"Maybe you can travel with us," Billy said eagerly, then added, "If it's okay with Ellie."

"Ellie's not sure she's speaking to Duke," she said, focusing on the buildings across the street.

"I hate cold winters," Duke continued without blinking an eye at her response. "The reason I left Nebraska to begin with. But a fall visit sounds nice right now."

"It is pretty in the fall, when everything turns gold." Billy gazed out the tent opening as if he could see it there.

Ellie sighed as she mixed dough. Why didn't Duke go away, now that he knew she wasn't speaking to him?

"And I'm thinking after that we'll go back to San Francisco and set up a business, at least for the winter. But I'm getting tired of saloons. Maybe a restaurant."

"You, start a restaurant? Can you cook?" Ellie scoffed before she remembered they weren't talking.

Duke grinned at her. "Well, no, but I know an excellent cook. She's standing right in front of me."

"I'm not going to San Francisco." She rolled out the dough vehemently, sprinkling flour on a sticky patch.

"Why not?" Duke let the question hang in the air for a moment. "Once you get Billy and the money back to your mama, why couldn't you get married and come to San Francisco with me? Or some other town, if you don't like San Francisco. Billy can help on the farm, there's not much work in the winter anyway. We can return to Nebraska in the spring, if you want."

Billy chuckled. "Can't see that Duke would be much help on the farm."

"I'm mighty good with horses, but I'm not much for bucking wheat," Duke admitted.

"Oh, I forgot about the livery." Billy laid out plates and forks.

"You sure there's nothing I can do for you this morning?" Duke asked.

"No, thank you," Ellie repeated.

"You know, the restaurant idea would be for my future wife. I'd help set it up and be the manager, but Ellie would be making all the decisions. She's proved herself to be a fine businesswoman."

Billy nodded while Ellie tried to focus on getting the apple slices laid evenly in the piecrusts.

"I wouldn't want to step on her toes, of course. Don't want her to lose her independence. I just want to share my life with her," Duke continued.

"I haven't said I'm going to marry you," Ellie said quietly, looking directly at Duke for the first time since he'd kissed her hand.

"I know that, but I'm hoping you'll change your mind," Duke answered as he gazed into her eyes. "I love you."

Ellie turned away, the warmth of her heart rushing into her face. "Do you have to say all this in front of my little brother?"

"Pardon my forwardness, but there's no parlor to take you to, and he knows all of this anyway. I might as well be honest."

"Honest!" Ellie set the pan on the table so hard a few apples flew out of it. "You haven't been honest! You've been manipulating me!"

"And you've been manipulating me," Duke answered quietly. "Your words and actions have turned this happy-go-lucky bartender into a respectable man who cares what people think of him, making him want to do the right thing. I wouldn't have gone to the meeting about Soapy Smith before I met you. And I wouldn't be tired of the saloon business, either. You see before you a changed man," he concluded as he spread his hands out.

Ellie stood dumbfounded. Had Duke's love for her created this change in him?

"Morning, Miss Ellie," a passerby called to her.

"Morning," Ellie said automatically, still staring at Duke. There was a pause as she pondered what Duke had said. Was he playacting for her benefit, or was he sincere?

Ellie shook her head. "Well, Mr. Masterson, I don't know how to respond to your speech."

"That's fine. Just think about it."

"And now we have customers." She indicated the line of men forming on the street, headed by Ralph and Jim.

"I will leave you to it, then." Duke took off his hat and swept it before her as he bowed, grasped her hand, and kissed it gently. She couldn't help but smile as he whispered, "My lovely Ellie," then watched as he sauntered down the street.

"I don't know what to do with that man."

"I can give you a hint," Billy said.

Ellie shook her head then put the top crusts on the next round of pies. She really didn't know what to think sometimes.

A CREW OF men set up in the street just outside the tent and started digging up the middle of the road.

"Is that the railroad we heard about?" Billy pointed to the workers as the next customer stepped forward.

"Yep. They're finishing the rail this week. Going to build the railroad down Broadway," the man explained as he took a piece of pie.

"Now that seems a strange place to put it," Ellie observed, remembering the railroad at the end of town in Red Cloud.

"I expect they're trying to make it easy on themselves, after building the rail next to the Dead Horse Trail," the man said.

"This must be much easier," she agreed, thinking of the steep ridges along the mountains. "I wish it wasn't such noisy work."

Ellie was used to the sounds of people coming and going every day, but the thumps of picks and shovels, and calls of the foremen took the din to a new level. On the other hand, quite a few of the crewmen came to buy pie during their lunch break, so the project had a silver lining.

THE REST OF the day passed quickly as Ellie and Billy worked. Ellie put the last set of pies in the stove as she pondered the day's events, especially Duke's speech about changing.

Her mind was on Duke as some customers serenaded her with a four-part harmony rendition of *Oh My Darling, Clementine*. It amazed her how the miners could hold a tune. Had they been in church choirs back home?

All that day, Ellie thought about Duke. He did seem sincere. And he did care about her, was even willing to change his business to one that suited her. But how could she be sure that their marriage would work? Men could promise one thing and end up doing something else, she knew. But somehow, she didn't think that Duke was that kind of man. He'd always done what he said he would.

"He really loves me," she breathed as she absently rubbed a burn on her finger.

"What?" Billy asked from the front table.

"Oh, nothing. Just talking to myself."

"Don't get crazy on me, now," he called back to her.

She laughed. "No, I won't."

"Good. Here you go, sir," Billy said to a miner as he gave him a plate of pie.

A CHILL HUNG in the air the next morning. "Getting close to fall," Billy mumbled as he slipped on his jacket.

"We're low on flour. You can watch the stove while I go borrow some from the hotel until the store opens. Anything else we need?"

"No. Say, 'Hi,' to everybody for me."

Ellie walked across to the hotel and met Ada at the door.

"Morning, how are you?"

"I'm fine, I guess."

Ada's eyes narrowed. "What's wrong?"

"I'm trying to decide if I want to marry Duke," she blurted out.

"But you love him?"

Ellie shook her head. "Ada, I only came in to borrow some flour."

"This is more important than flour," Ada said as she grabbed her elbow and steered Ellie to the parlor sofa. "Sit down. You need to think about this. You love him, but you don't want to marry him? Why?"

"You know what it's like to be a woman. I've watched my mother and neighbors my whole life. All they do is dote on their husbands and children, and they never have a thought for themselves. I don't know if I want to do that."

"But you're missing one benefit of married life. It's *rewarding* to live for your family, too, for something bigger than yourself. And good married couples are like partners where the wife gives her thoughts on matters, too. Do you know who wanted to build this hotel?" She leaned forward.

"You did?"

"Yes, it was my idea," Ada said. "And my husband went along with *me*, not the other way around."

"Hmm," Ellie said as she looked at the photographs on the parlor wall. The faces of Ada and Tom looked down at her encouragingly. She hadn't thought of it quite like that. Duke was offering her a partnership with the restaurant. "Partners."

"Yes, it works well. Think about it."

"If I promise to, can I borrow some flour until the store opens?"

Ada laughed. "Oh, all right. Come on into the kitchen."

A DREAM OF Ellie lingering in his mind, Duke woke with a grin on his face. Planning to see her as soon as he got cleaned up, he rolled over and glanced at Dan in the cot across from his.

Dan was lying in bed, shaking, as sweat shone on his freckled skin.

Duke knelt down next to him and felt the heat rising off Dan's forehead before he touched him. "Dan?" he asked softly. "Can you hear me?"

"Duke?" He opened his watering eyes. "I don't feel too good."

"Just stay right there. I'll fetch the doctor."

Duke threw on some clothes and ran down the street to Doc Loman's house. Dan looked so weak, and he'd never seen someone with such a high fever before. There'd been a typhoid epidemic in California a few years ago.

Please, God, don't let it be that, he thought as he rapped on the door.

"Doc? You up yet?"

A tousled head appeared at a bedroom window. "Who's there?"

"Doc, it's Duke. Dan Palmer's real sick."

"Hang on. I'll be right down," the doctor called, before pulling his head back inside. Soon, Doc Loman had his black bag in hand and was heading to the Frisco.

THE WOODCUTTING LAD appeared at the pie tent the next morning, battered hat in hand. "Hello, Miss Ellie."

"Hello." She gave him a polite smile.

His fair, blond hair waved in the breeze as he asked, "Anything I can do for you today?"

"We still have a fair amount of wood, thank you. What's your name?"

"Nathan."

"Do you live nearby, Nathan?"

"Yes, ma'am. Just over that way." He pointed toward Dyea.

"Come back in a few days to chop some wood, if you still want to by then."

"Oh, I will. I'll be back." Nathan beamed as if she'd made him the next president of the United States. "Thank you, Miss Ellie."

"Have a nice day." She smiled at him, then turned away to put a batch of pies in the oven. She didn't understand boys or men. Why Nathan would get all excited over chopping wood she didn't know. But she'd get more wood for the stove.

Billy served the next customers as Ellie made another batch of pies, wondering where Duke was. She hadn't seen him today. Her mind went to scenes from the past—his proposal, bringing Billy home from the bar, his speech about changing. All his compassion, responsibility, and love for her shone in her memory. Here she was edging toward saying yes to his proposal, and he wasn't even there to appreciate it.

A tall man in dungarees nodded at her. "Great pie, miss."

She smiled at him. "Thank you." At least the pie business was doing well.

ELLIE WAS DISAPPOINTED when Duke didn't come see her by the third morning. She'd gotten used to seeing his smile at the beginning of every day. It didn't seem right for him to be away for so long. It left a big hole in her life, a hole no one else could fill.

The racket made by the railroad crew decreased. Instead of laying the rails, the men were adding gravel near the ends of the ties so that traffic could pass on level with the tracks. She heard the gravel swish in the shovels and beat down on the wooden ties.

The foreman tipped his hat when she stood in the tent entrance.

"Morning, Miss Ellie. Hope we aren't in your way."

"Not at all." Ellie smiled at him. "Would you like some pie?"

"Not today, thanks, miss. We need to have this rail to the depot finished by tonight. Got to get ready for the big opening tomorrow."

The morning was the same as most for Ellie—rolling out dough, making pies, baking, and serving her customers. The line was a little shorter now, as some of the more unlucky miners had started to leave for home.

Ellie's thoughts strayed to Duke at times. She loved him and he loved her. Maybe that would be enough to build a future together. She wished she could talk to him right now.

"Still the best pie in Alaska," Ralph said to her.

"Still the best," Jim echoed.

"Thank you, gentlemen." She was going to miss those two when she left Skagway.

Nathan appeared at the tent door, hat in hand. "Good afternoon, Miss Ellie. Do you need any more wood?"

Pointing at the decimated woodpile, she said, "Yes, thank you. The ax is over there."

"Yes, ma'am." Nathan went right to work.

He spent the next hour chopping wood as she and Billy went on serving their customers. The steady *womp, womp* sounded as he split logs with the regularity of a ticking grandfather clock. Soon she stopped consciously hearing it, only noticing when Nathan slowed down for a moment.

He certainly has stamina, she thought as he put the ax down and started stacking the wood without taking a break. *He has done a lot of work. Maybe I'll offer him a free piece of pie when he's finished.*

When Nathan appeared in the doorway, Ellie was alone at the pie stand.

"I'm finished with the wood, Miss Ellie."

"Thank you. You did a nice job," Ellie said as she glanced at the neat pile. "Would you like some pie? I have one piece left in this pan."

Nathan bounced on his toes and wrung his hat in his hands. His mouth worked a moment before any words came out. "Oh, Miss Ellie, thank you. Yes, I would!"

She smiled and handed him a plate. He inhaled the pie, and then looked up at her.

"Miss Ellie, I've been thinking, I mean—" He edged closer to her. She was suddenly aware of how strong he was when he grabbed her arm. "Would you be my girl?" he breathed as he bent down toward her.

Ellie stepped back as she yelped, "No!" Then she recovered from the shock and said to him more politely, "Sorry, Nathan, I'm spoken for."

As he realized his mistake, Nathan's face turned red. "I thought, with the pie—"

"You're a very nice boy, and a good woodcutter, but Duke Masterson and I are courting," she concluded as Nathan let go of her arm.

Nathan fled when Billy entered the tent.

Her brother looked after him with raised eyebrows. "What was that about?"

"He, uh, wanted me to be his girl."

"Oh. Well, at least he has good taste."

Ellie thought about the incident with Nathan as she stoked the wood stove. She'd told him she was with Duke and she'd meant it when she said it.

No matter how hard she'd fought it, she had to admit that she and Duke were a couple—they cared about the same things, and had made a good team when they had to deal with Soapy Smith.

Where was Duke, anyway? Why hadn't he stopped by today? Ellie's mind raced through many scenarios—from Duke changing his mind, to his being ill, to his being shot by a drunken merrymaker with an errant pistol.

All were unlikely, she knew, but she did wonder. She considered going to his saloon that evening to see what was going on, but her pride prevented her from following through with that idea, not wanting to look like a lovesick puppy needing attention. She was independent, and wasn't that one thing that Duke liked about her—that she could take care of herself? Well, she'd just keep doing that until Duke had the time to come by and explain his absence.

In the meantime, she missed him and hoped he was all right.

CHAPTER TEN

DUKE GENTLY DABBED his partner's forehead with the cool, damp towel as Dan's eyes flickered open. "Hey, partner. You're awake. How you feeling?"

Dan smiled weakly. "A little better. Why aren't you bartending or kissing Ellie?"

"You're more important. Don't worry. Ralph and Jim are running the bar for us. Now, the doc wants you to drink this stuff." Duke poured a spoonful from a brown bottle and supported Dan's head as he took the medicine.

"What's he say?"

"You had a high fever, but it's coming down. Your job is to rest and he'll check on you again tonight."

"Can I have some water?"

"Sure, coming right up." Duke brought him a glass. He remembered the way Ellie sipped water after their first kiss and was surprised that he hadn't heard from her. However, he was also afraid that Ellie would catch whatever sickness this was and was glad to keep her away until the danger passed, or the doctor was sure that it wasn't contagious.

Duke had stayed by Dan's bed, afraid to leave him until the fever broke. Maybe he could get a message to her tonight by the doctor, once he came back to check on Dan. Duke would write her a quick note, just so she wouldn't wonder where he was and why he hadn't stopped by to see her. Now that she'd finally come around a little, he didn't want to mess things up with a misunderstanding.

BILLY AND ELLIE were selling pies as fast as they could make them as customers stopped at the tent on their way to the depot. The White Pass and Yukon Route Railroad was celebrating the new route opening that day. People could board at the depot, by the dock, and ride the train down the street and all the way up the pass now. It was a fine morning with a brisk breeze coming down the valley toward the bay, the street busy with men heading to the wharf.

"Good business today," Billy winked at Ellie. "Nice way to end our season."

Ellie took a quick breath as she realized he was right. Soon, they'd be leaving Skagway for home. Her heart thudded as it occurred to her she could leave with Duke at her side.

"Are you going to the depot?" a boy asked. Ellie looked up to see Robert holding Ada's hand.

Ellie smiled down at him. "No, but we'll see the train when it passes here."

Ada laughed. "It'll be hard to miss, that's for sure! Well, we'll see you later, then." She took Tom's hand in her other one, and the family formed a chain with linked hands. Their line stretched halfway across the street, and people smiled at them as they stepped out of the way.

"Have fun," Ellie called as they started down the street, tucking a stray wisp of hair behind her ear as the breeze mussed her bun.

"Maybe you and Duke will have a family like that," Billy mused.

Ellie nodded as she imagined being in Ada's place. The thumping of her heart showed how much she wanted that. She wondered again where Duke was.

The line of pie customers dwindled, and Ellie heard the train whistle sounding its call. Then the train, festooned with red, white, and blue bunting, steamed its way down the street. Cars were packed with passengers and hundreds of arms waved through the windows. Billy and Ellie laughed and waved in return.

"Too bad Duke isn't here to see this," Billy commented. "He's not usually one to miss a celebration."

"Yes, I've been wondering where he is," Ellie admitted as they watched the caboose of the train pass by, steam billowing behind it.

"I'm sure he has good reason to be away." Billy touched her shoulder, then went back to washing dishes.

"Oh, I'm not worried about it." Ellie picked up a pie pan as her stomach tightened. Being gone for a day was one thing, but several days was highly unusual. Had he changed his mind? Was it his turn to get cold feet?

"Want me to go by the saloon?"

"No."

Billy kept quiet as he scrubbed a pie pan.

DOC LOMAN STOPPED by the tent, an envelope in his hand.

"Evenin' Miss Ellie. Duke Masterson asked me to bring this to you."

Ellie's hands were shaking as she opened the letter.

Dear Ellie,

Dan has been very sick. I've been tending to him, trying to get his fever to go down. It finally broke today, and he should be well soon. Then I'll come see you.

I've had a lot of time to sit and think about you. I hear your laughter in my mind. I wish I could see your brilliant smile and taste those sweet lips. But for now, I'll content myself with thoughts of you. I hope our last conversation had the positive effect on you as it did on me. I look forward to entering married life as your partner, becoming closer as we get to know each other better, and supporting each other as we chase our dreams. It won't be long now. After waiting my whole life for you, a few days are not too long to wait.

All my love,
Duke

Ellie pressed the letter to her chest and exhaled, realizing that she'd been holding her breath. He still loved her. He'd just been nursing Dan back to health. Now that she knew, she wasn't surprised. It was so like Duke to be generous to his business partner and friend.

The word partner brought her back to the letter. He wanted to be partners with her. Wasn't that what Ada said about a good marriage? That it was like being partners? Ada was right—she and Duke could be partners in marriage. And in life.

Ellie read the letter again. As the words flowed, images came to her mind. Duke managing the restaurant as she ran the kitchen.

Holding a baby in her arms as Duke cooed over her shoulder. Duke with gray hair, smiling down at her. Suddenly, she wanted everything that marriage with Duke would offer. She wanted to be his partner, to grow old with him.

She set the letter on the bench and picked up her shawl. "Dan's been sick. I'm going to Duke's," she called to Billy.

"Okay," he replied, picking up the letter as she left the tent.

A COOL WIND was blowing from the north that night, and the sky was a sapphire blue as she pulled the shawl tightly around her shoulders. Ellie could see the lantern's light as she approached the living quarters tent behind the saloon. She entered quietly, so she wouldn't wake Dan if he were asleep. Duke was bent over Dan, gently dabbing his face with a cloth, more gentle than she'd ever seen him.

He looked up. The light from the lantern gave his face a golden glow as he stood and smiled at her. Ellie placed her hand in his, his warmth stealing up her arm. They spoke quietly to each other, so as not to wake Dan.

"Ellie," he breathed as he drew her close.

"Duke." Ellie glanced at Dan sleeping on the cot. "How is he?"

"Better." He beamed as he looked into her eyes.

"I'm so glad." She let her eyes remain on his.

"I'm so sorry not to give you word sooner, but I was afraid it might be contagious and I didn't want to leave him—" Duke began to explain.

She shook her head. "It's all right. You don't have to apologize for being a good friend."

Dan stirred and they both started toward him. His eyes opened and Dan saw her. "Ellie."

She bent over him and felt his forehead, which was warm, but not alarmingly so. "Hi, Dan. You just rest there."

"That's all he'll let me do."

Ellie turned to Duke and saw the lines on his face. "I can watch him for a little while, if you want to take a nap or something."

"No, thank you. I'm doing fine." He smiled tenderly, his eyes sparkling in the lantern light.

She looked at the men for a moment, at a loss for what to do next. It didn't seem right to be chatting in a sick room, and she wasn't needed to help out. "Well, guess I better get back to Billy, then."

Duke put his hands in his pockets. "Oh, all right."

"But, Duke?" She stepped toward him.

"Yes?"

"What you said in the letter, I want those things, too."

"My darling," he whispered as he swept her up in his arms.

She hugged him close in reply.

"Will you marry me?"

"Yes. Yes, I will."

He kissed her, gently at first, then more deeply as their lips melded together. A rush of heat coursed through her body as she let herself relax in his arms. She couldn't think of any place she'd rather be, any moment she wanted to last longer than this one. Then he stepped back and their eyes met again.

"I love you, Ellie," he said as he gazed down at her.

"I-I love you too," she breathed. Then she remembered where they were, drew back, and pulled her shawl around her. "Good night."

"Good night, my darling."

She could swear her feet didn't touch the ground as she walked back to the tent. She felt like she was floating on the breeze that stirred the birch leaves and sent them fluttering in the darkening sky. Duke's kiss played on her lips, and Ellie knew that all was right in the world.

Ellie woke up with a smile on her face, fresh from dreaming about Duke holding her closely, whispering sweet nothings in her ear. Then she remembered that she'd accepted his proposal yesterday, and her stomach churned.

"What have I done?" she murmured.

"Did you say something?" Billy asked as he buttoned his shirt.

"I can't believe I said yes to him," Ellie explained as she quickly dressed in the cool morning air.

"Why not? You love each other. You're just having cold feet this morning," Billy said as he lit the fire.

Ellie's fingers worked furiously as she wove her hair into a bun. "I never expected to get married, at least, not like this. I can't go around accepting proposals from bartenders."

"Now, Ellie, you're sounding like a snob." Billy's voice had an edge in it for the first time she could remember. "I'm disappointed in you, and Mama would be too. There's nothing wrong with any honest job, so don't get your nose in the air." He thrust a log on the fire in the stove. "That's no reason not to marry somebody."

"Oh, I don't know. That's not it really…" Ellie let the sentence hang unfinished, as she wasn't sure to what she was objecting. Everything had happened so fast this summer. The speed of it was the problem. She hadn't meant to fall in love, but Duke was so charming, and here she was engaged to him. What if all his sweet talk was only that, talk, and she ended up dependent on his whims? Would Duke be any different from other men?

"He loves you and he'll make a good life for you," Billy told her with the same edge in his voice. "Now quit the cold feet and stop worrying about it." Then he grabbed the bucket and went for water.

Ellie stared after him, tongue-tied. Where had that voice of authority come from? Billy was certainly not a little boy from Nebraska anymore.

"WHAT ARE YOU daydreaming about?" Dan teased as he stacked glasses next to him.

"I am *not* daydreaming," Duke said.

Dan grinned. "You've been wiping that part of the bar for quite a while now. Thinking about someone we know?"

"Yes," Duke admitted. "Now that she's said yes, I need to make sure she doesn't change her mind."

Dan laughed. "I suppose it doesn't hurt to be sure, in this case. Well, what's important to her?"

"Money for her family."

"So what can you give her that's related to that?"

Duke thought for a moment then his heart leapt in his chest. "I could pay for her ship tickets, and that would give her more money to take home to her mama." He slapped Dan on the back. "That's perfect!"

"Give her flowers with the tickets, and make it more romantic."

"What a great idea, I'll do it! But wait—" Duke looked at his pocket watch. "Do you think it's too early to buy tickets today?"

"Well, go and find out. I'll watch the place."

"Thanks!" Duke called over his shoulder as he ran out.

"GOOD MORNING!" DUKE'S voice was even more cheerful than usual.

"Hey, Duke!" Billy called from behind the tent.

"Morning." Ellie smiled as she tied her apron strings.

Duke offered her an envelope and a bunch of flowers.

"Why, Duke, where did you find sweet peas in Skagway?" She took them gently and inhaled their sweet scent.

"Arnie Arneson has them in front of his house. Said I could have some."

"They're lovely," Ellie said as she looked for a container to put them in.

"There's something else, too." Duke handed her the envelope.

She set the flowers on the table and opened the envelope. "Oh, Duke!" Her hand flew to her heart.

"My present to you, so you can save more money to give to your mama," Duke explained.

"Oh, my!" Ellie hugged him. The warmth and strength of his arms felt so inviting that she stayed there for a moment. She stepped back and explained to her brother. "It's two tickets to Seattle."

"Gosh, thanks, Duke!" Billy clapped him on the back.

She stood with her hand over her racing heart, blinking tears from her eyes. "I don't know what to say."

"Well, say you'll accept them."

"Okay, we accept." Ellie nodded as she swept the tears from her cheeks. "And thank you."

"You're welcome." Duke grinned his little boy smile.

"When's it for?" Billy asked.

"August fourth, a little more than a week away."

"So soon," she murmured, looking at the tickets.

"I get the impression we're both doing well, about ready to go," Duke said. He raised his eyebrows. "Is it too soon? I can change them."

"No. I am so sick of pie," Billy answered. "Let's go then."

Ellie laughed. "You're right. I am pretty sick of pie, too!"

They all laughed for a moment.

"Duke." Ellie turned to him. She looked into his clear blue eyes. Something soft yet strong drew her in as she gazed into them, and she thought she could trust him to do anything for her. Her heart pounded harder, as she lost herself in those eyes and his arms gently wrapped around her waist.

"Ellie? You still say yes?" he asked softly.

She was sure as she nodded. "Yes. I say yes."

Billy's whoop reminded them that he was still there. Duke laughed and they shook hands.

"Congratulations!" Billy grinned. "Wait 'til we write Mama and tell her she's getting a son-in-law!"

"I hope she likes you," Ellie said. Until now, she'd only thought of the impact on her own life. Her marriage would affect everyone else in her family, too. And Mama was bound to have a strong opinion about it, like she did with everything else.

"Oh, she'll like him all right." Billy slapped Duke on the back again. "Especially if he helps out with the horses."

She hoped he was right. If not, this would be a very unpleasant trip home.

Dear Mama,

An extraordinary thing has happened. I have become engaged. The gentleman's name is Duke Masterson. He was raised in Red Cloud and his father still owns the livery stable there.

We met on the ship on the way to Skagway. He has been very helpful to us while we've worked here in town. He is charming, and enjoys books and music. I think you will like him very much.

At least she hoped so. It would be disastrous if Mama didn't like him. But Ellie was sure that Duke could bring Mama around with a little time.

She continued writing.

Duke is currently running a saloon in Skagway, but has been living in San Francisco for the past few years. Our plan, if it is all right with you, is to get married on our return to Nebraska and help out on the farm this fall, then go to San Francisco for the winter. Duke does not like the cold winters and we plan to open a restaurant there. Then we can come back home to visit later.

We have made enough money for the mortgage, and still have some left over, and I'm thankful that all our work is paying off to help you keep the farm. I am looking forward to seeing you again. Our ship leaves on August fourth and we should be home a few weeks after that.

Love, Ellie

P. S. Billy sends his love. You will be pleased to see how much he has grown into a man during our stay here.

Ellie placed the letter in the envelope and sealed it, then stood. "I'm going to the post office."

"Okay, sis. See if you can get some apples on the way back."

"Oh, yes. Thanks for reminding me."

Ellie walked to the post office, barely noticing people as they passed her on the boardwalk. Her mind was on one thing— marriage. She was going to do it! She was really going to marry Duke Masterson. She was surprised she felt so calm about it. Maybe that was because it was the right thing to do. She smiled as she thought of how happy Ada would be at the news.

CHAPTER ELEVEN

ADA SQUEALED AND hugged Ellie. "I'm so glad you're finally getting married!"

Ellie laughed. "Well, it's your doing, you know."

"I don't mind getting credit for it." Ada clapped her hands. "Let's plan a wedding!"

"But I thought we'd get married in Nebraska." Ellie fingered her cameo.

"No, you can't cheat me out of a wedding that easily. Get married with us first, and then have a second ceremony with your folks."

"Well, I guess I could ask Duke—"

"You don't think Duke is going to turn down a reason to celebrate with his Skagway friends, do you?"

Ellie laughed. "No, you're right. We're leaving town on Thursday. Can we get a preacher for Wednesday?"

Ellie's hand rested on Duke's arm as they strolled down the boardwalk toward the preacher's house.

Hesitating a moment, Duke said with a sheepish grin, "Um, there's one more thing I should tell you, before the wedding ceremony."

She stopped and glared at him. "Something else you should have told me?"

"My Christian name is not Duke."

Relief sank into her shoulders. "Oh. I figured that was a nickname."

"My real name is Alfonse."

"Oh my." Ellie suppressed the giggle rising in her throat. "Where did that come from?"

"My mother read it in a book and thought it sounded nice."

"Well, I guess that gives me a lot of latitude when I name our son one day."

They laughed as they rounded the corner to Reverend Simpson's house. With Duke's good looks, it was inevitable they would have pretty babies. She squeezed his arm again while he knocked on the door.

Reverend Simpson answered, his wispy hair combed away from his fair face. "Yes?"

Duke cleared his throat. "Reverend, we'd like to talk to you about getting married."

"How delightful! Please, come in."

They were ushered into the parlor. The reverend shook their hands, and then indicated the red, upholstered sofa. He beamed as his face turned pink with excitement.

"I get to do a lot of funerals, but very few weddings in this town. I would be honored to officiate."

"Thank you, sir," Ellie said. "Could we get married next Wednesday?"

"Certainly. That evening, so working folks can attend?"

Duke nodded. "That sounds good."

"How nice, a wedding! Let's have some tea and cookies to celebrate." Reverend Simpson rubbed his hands together as he headed for the kitchen. "Do you take milk or sugar?"

ELLIE AND ADA had stopped to ask Arne Arneson if they could have some flowers from his garden for the wedding. Now they were on the way to the general store to buy a wedding dress.

Conrad Buxton peered at Ellie through his spectacles, his head cocked to one side, his bald head giving him the appearance of a cue ball. "Well, Miss Ellie, I suggest one of these gowns for the occasion." He proudly laid out a couple on the counter—one pink satin and one lavender damask.

Ellie shook her head vehemently. "Too much. I don't want to look like a dance hall girl at my wedding." When he gave her a sour look, she added softly, "Do you have something less, ah, showy?"

"Maybe a nice calico or muslin?" Ada suggested.

He sighed as he carefully folded the gowns, put them away, and laid out two dresses, a forget-me-not blue calico and a soft-pink paisley.

Ellie brushed the calico with her hand. She liked the fabric and it would do for other occasions later.

"Perfect." Ada nodded. "The blue will show off your complexion nicely."

As she held it up against herself, Ellie beamed. It was a good fit except for being too long.

Ada smiled at Ellie. "With a little hemming, it'll be perfect."

"We'll take it," she announced.

He puffed up his rotund chest. "I knew that would be the one. Just knew it."

"Thank you, Mr. Buxton," Ellie said. Who knew it'd be so easy to find a wedding dress?

"DO I GET to see it?" Duke asked.

"Of course not. You'll have to wait for the wedding," Ellie replied lightly as she squeezed his arm. They ambled toward the wharf, people smiling at them as they passed.

"Congratulations, you two," Ralph said as he shook Duke's hand.

"Thank you," Duke said.

"Congratulations," Jim echoed.

"May I kiss the bride?" Ralph asked.

Duke nodded as Ralph gave Ellie a little kiss on the cheek.

"May you have a wonderful life together," Ralph said.

Jim kissed Ellie's cheek shyly.

"Thank you, gentlemen." Ellie had a lump in her throat as she smiled at her best customers. Then they continued down the street.

"So, we have a church, a minister, and a dress. Ada and Tom are giving us a night in the hotel after the reception. Have we forgotten anything?" Ellie asked.

Duke stopped and turned toward her. His blue eyes were as deep as the sea. "I have you...what else could I possibly need?"

Ellie's heart thumped harder in her breast. His face moved toward her, but Ellie stopped his progress when she put her hand up.

"Not here, in front of all these people."

Duke laughed and settled for a peck on her cheek. "Yes, ma'am. Whatever you wish is my command."

Ellie stood in front of the mirror, wedding dress on, while Ada hemmed.

"Hold still," Ada said through the pins pinched between her lips. "There, does that look even?"

Ellie looked at the reflection of the dress hem in the mirror. "Yes, I think so."

Ada took the pins out of her mouth and smiled as she rose from the floor. "You do look lovely in it."

Ellie raised her gaze to see herself in the mirror and couldn't help beaming. White lace accented her neck, wrists, and waist. She was lovely—and happy. Her bosom heaved as she took a deep breath, trying to relieve some of the full feeling there. It didn't work.

"I am so glad you're getting married before you leave," Ada said.

"I am, too." Ellie grinned. "I had to be talked into it at first, but, now it seems so natural to have a ceremony here, with you, and Dan, and everyone else we know in Skagway."

"The whole town is talking about it. People are asking to contribute something for the reception. I don't know if the hotel's going to hold everybody. But it'll be a great party, I'm sure of that."

Ellie shook her head at the idea. "Who'd have guessed a farm girl like me would have so much fuss made over her?"

"It's your winning personality and your pies," Ada said. "Of course, it doesn't hurt that you're marrying one of the most popular men in town. Duke is a charmer."

"He is that. And to think I thought him a boor when I first met him. I had no idea then how fond of him I'd become." She couldn't stop smiling.

"And now you're getting married—husband and wife the rest of your days. Just goes to show you, life never turns out the way you expect."

"True. Sometimes it turns out even better."

Ada hugged her. "Now, get out of that dress and let me hem it up for you."

ELLIE STOOD FOR a moment, staring at the bare space between the trees that had been her home most of the summer. Billy had already sold or given away their stove, tent, equipment, and anything else they didn't need for their trip or back home. If she looked closely, she could see the smudged burn marks on the ground where the heat had spread through the stove feet.

Her lower back twinged as she remembered all the hours she'd spent on her feet there. She rubbed it absently, but smiled at the memory of all the kind customers, the gentlemen who went out of their way to support the business while treating her like a young lady.

A stream of faces formed in her mind's eye—dark and light-skinned, beards and clean-shaven chins, strong men and weak, taciturn and chatty. Ralph and Jim, Frank Thompson. The railroad crew. The English gentleman at Dyea.

Bobby Joe's face came to her mind, and she recalled laughing with him about gumbo before they went over the rapids. So many dead because of the gold rush, others going home broke or broken.

She thought of Rose and Johnny and tears came to her eyes. It wasn't fair. What had given her and Billy the right to survive when so many hadn't?

"A penny for your thoughts," Duke said softly as he put his arm around her waist.

"I'm just thinking about those who didn't make it." Duke squeezed her closer. "It isn't fair that Billy and I got so far and they didn't."

Duke gently turned Ellie around to face him. His blue eyes were piercing as he spoke quietly, but with conviction in his voice. "Ellie, some of it is dumb luck which nobody can explain. But I think part of it is your good characters and your pure hearts. They *earned* you the right to survive. God wanted you two to be here today. And I'm pretty grateful you are."

Another tear rolled down her cheek, and her heart was too full to speak louder than a whisper. "Thank you."

His kiss was as soft as a cloud, yet warm and comforting at the same time. She couldn't imagine a better place to be than in his arms.

"Come on, you two lovers, let's get this luggage over to the hotel," Billy called.

Duke chuckled as he grabbed a trunk. "Oh, all right." Ellie turned and wiped her face before Billy could see she'd been crying. She and Billy had rooms at the hotel the night before the wedding.

A MAN COULDN'T ask for a better group to attend his bachelor party. Duke was grateful to Dan for getting them all together.

"A toast." Duke raised his glass. "To Dan, the best friend a guy ever had."

His partner nodded as the men around the saloon table drank, and then raised his own glass. "And to my best friend, may his wedding and marriage be as great as he deserves."

"Hear, hear," echoed off the copper-tiled ceiling before they all drank to Duke. A regular customer with a white, handlebar mustache pounded on the table in agreement.

"So, Duke, what are your plans after the wedding?" Tom asked while the bartender poured another round of whiskey.

"Well, first we'll have a little honeymoon on the ship." He grinned as the men murmured at the mention of *honeymoon*. "Then we'll go back to Nebraska to deposit Billy and the money, and have a second ceremony."

"You're in big trouble if her mama doesn't like you." Dan slapped him on his shoulder and the men laughed.

"But I bet she'll think you're grand," Ralph said.

"Grand," Jim echoed. "All the ladies love you."

Heads nodded in agreement.

"But you won't stay in Nebraska, will you?" the gentleman with the mustache asked.

"No, no." He waved the question off. "No, we'll go to San Francisco and spend the winter there."

Tom raised his glass. "To soft weather."

"To rain pitter-pattering on the roof," Duke agreed. He could almost hear it already.

Dan teased, "Maybe little feet pitter-pattering on the floor before too long." The men roared with laughter.

"You'll be a good father one day," Tom offered.

"Thank you, my good man." Duke took another sip of whiskey. "I hope to be."

Ralph set his glass down. "Are you coming back next summer?"

"Come back next summer," Jim said.

"They say there's a gold strike in Nome. Could make a fortune up there," Ralph said.

Duke thought seriously for a moment, then nodded. "If Ellie wants to come back. If *she* wants to."

"Ah, henpecked already!" the old gentleman teased, and the group chortled.

Dan shook his head. "No, just in love."

Duke grinned and nodded. "Yes, madly in love. Here boys, have another round on me!" he replied to their chuckles.

"YOU DON'T THINK the flowers are too much?" Ellie said as she fingered the sprigs of forget-me-nots on the table, ready to be woven into her hair.

"On the contrary, it'll make you look more like a bride," Ada assured her as she took the wedding dress from the ironing board. "Here, put this on."

Ellie slipped into it, and then held still while Ada fastened the tiny buttons on the back of the dress. She put on her cameo necklace, thinking of Papa and Mama. It seemed so long ago that they had given it to her. She wished they could see her all grown up now. At least Mama would soon, and be proud of what Ellie and Billy had accomplished this summer.

Ellie glanced at the iron and ironing board, thinking back to the captain's tea on the ship when she was so anxious to please, and wishing she'd had an iron. She couldn't help but giggle at how foolish she'd been.

Ada winked at her. "Thinking about tonight?"

"No!" Her face turned hot at the mention of the wedding night. "When we were on the ship coming here, Billy and I were invited to tea with the captain. And I was so sorry I didn't have an iron to touch up my traveling suit."

"And now your wedding dress is all ironed and you don't need to impress anybody," Ada said.

Ellie nodded. "I've talked with paupers and millionaires since then, and I learned that irons are not what's important."

Ada nodded. "No, it's what's inside."

"The content of your character," Ellie concluded.

"And you've proven your worth." Ada picked up a flower and wove it into Ellie's loose bun of dark hair, then another. "That's lovely. Now turn around."

Ellie looked in the mirror. Her reflection appeared as happy as she felt, and she hugged Ada. "Thank you."

"Oh, my pleasure. I wouldn't miss this for anything."

There was a knock at the door. "Sis, you ready yet?"

"Just about," Ellie called back.

"Well, hurry up. You don't want to be late."

"All right, we're coming!" Ada sang out.

She opened the door for Billy, who wore a borrowed black suit, looking much older than Ellie expected.

"You look pretty!" her brother said.

"Thanks, Billy. You're looking awful handsome yourself," Ellie said as she blinked the tears back. Suddenly Billy looked like a younger version of Papa. If only Papa could have been here to give her away.

"We'll have a hard time keeping the ladies away from you today," Ada teased.

Billy blushed and offered his arm to Ellie. "To the church?"

"Yes, to the church!" Ellie placed her arm on his.

AS THE ORGANIST played *The Wedding March*, Ada and Dan walked down the aisle toward Duke, who looked tall, handsome, and debonair in his fine suit and embroidered waistcoat. Then Ellie held Billy's arm and stepped to the edge of the church's threshold. The full feeling back in her chest, she took a deep breath and Billy kissed her cheek softly.

"You're beautiful, Ellie," he murmured.

"Thank you," Ellie whispered. "You're quite the grown man today." He patted her hand and butterflies fluttered in her stomach. Then Ellie and Billy walked down the aisle.

Rows of familiar faces smiled as she passed by: Ralph, Jim, the postmaster, Buxton from the store, pie customers, and railroad workers. It looked like the whole town was packed into the pews today.

"Who gives this woman in marriage?" Reverend Simpson asked.

"I do," Billy said solemnly. Then Billy gave her hand to Duke. Duke's smile was a broad grin yet his eyes were serious. He looked deep into her eyes while the preacher spoke.

"Alfonse Masterson, do you take this woman to be your lawfully wedded wife, to have and to hold from this day forward, for better or worse, in sickness and in health, until death do you part?"

"I do," he answered clearly.

Ellie's sight blurred with tears. She wasn't sure what emotion to call it—pride, joy, love. But she knew that she was grateful to be there with Duke.

"Eleanor Webster, do you take this man to be your lawfully wedded husband, to have and to hold from this day forward, for better or worse, in sickness and in health, until death do you part?"

"I do," Ellie answered with all the conviction she could muster into those two words. She never felt so sure of anything as she did at that moment. Duke was the right person to be with for the rest of her life.

"You may kiss the bride."

Duke kissed her lightly on her lips, then picked her up and swung her around in a circle while the crowd whooped its approval. She laughed as he set her back down. He gallantly offered his arm to her. "My darling?"

She put her arm on his. "My love." And they walked down the aisle, to the applause of the onlookers.

DUKE'S CHEST FILLED with pride as Ellie shook hands with yet another pie customer, as if she stood in reception lines all her life. She looked like a princess in her wedding dress and with flowers in her hair. No wonder the men were fawning all over her. He was a lucky man.

Tom said, "Congratulations, Ellie."

"Thank you." She smiled graciously.

"Alfonse, eh?" Tom winked at him.

"Now you know why I go by Duke."

"Duke, this is Nathan, the woodcutter," Ellie introduced the young man.

Duke shook his hand. "Ah, appreciate your helping at the pie tent."

"Congratulations, Miss Ellie, I mean Mrs..." Nathan faltered.

"Thank you, Nathan," Ellie said quickly.

The reception line included the whole town. Duke was glad to see them gathered to show their respect for Ellie, even if he did have to smile and say thank you hundreds of times. He didn't mind sharing Ellie with them now. But it was him she was going upstairs with tonight. He felt the stirring in his body at that thought.

It was Duke that was going on the ship with her tomorrow—going everywhere with her from now on. He had wooed and won her, and nothing was going to stop him from making her the happiest woman on the planet.

He was going to be the best husband and father in the history of man. Starting now—tonight—they would be the most loving, most faithful married couple since Odysseus and Penelope. And he wouldn't have to take a voyage to prove it. No, he wasn't planning to leave Ellie's side—ever—for the rest of his life.

"Duke?" Ellie was looking at him with a puzzled expression.

"Yes, my love?"

"Ada was just talking to you. Are you all right?"

"I've never been better. Never," he added as he held her hand to his lips and kissed it. She shivered in response and he answered with his own tremor.

"Me, neither," she replied.

ELLIE REGARDED THE green and white mountains gliding by the steamship and breathed in the crisp air. She felt Duke's arms enclose her waist from behind. This time, she was expecting it.

"Can't get enough of this scenery, can you?"

"It is beautiful," she murmured.

He chuckled. "Not like where we're headed, so we might as well enjoy it."

"Duke, do you think we'll come back one day?"

"To Alaska?" He pointed at the glaciers on the peaks above them, glimmers of blue peeking out from the white snow. "If you want to. I wouldn't mind if *you* want to."

She nodded. "Maybe. If I don't have to bake any more pies."

Duke laughed and turned her toward him. "My love, you never have to bake another pie as long as you live, if that's your wish." He kissed her on her nose.

She giggled. "Never?"

"The only thing I require of you is to love me, and let me love you in return."

"That sounds pretty easy to do."

"We have a lifetime and a whole world ahead of us," Duke murmured in her ear as they embraced.

"A whole world ahead of us," she repeated as she turned her face to his. Their kiss was slow and sweet as their lips met and melded together once, twice. His lips traveled to her forehead and left another kiss there. She sighed and looked into his deep-blue eyes.

"Duke."

"Yes, my love?"

"Thanks for falling in love with me."

He laughed softly. "No, thank you for being so wonderful. I'm going to make you the happiest woman in the world."

"I believe that," Ellie said. "I believe it."

EPILOGUE

Nebraska

MAMA STOOD ON the front porch, arms crossed, studying Duke's face as if memorizing it. "So, you're Duke. As you might have guessed, I've been doing some asking about you in town."

With hands behind him as he stood at attention, his smile seemed a little fixed under his mother-in-law's scrutiny. "Yes, ma'am."

Ellie hoped he held up under Mama's gaze. She'd seen it bring down grown men before.

"The frog incident I'll put down to youthful exuberance. No bad stories about you or your family. And you look all right." Mama put her hands on her hips as she kept staring at Duke. "Do you really love my daughter?"

"I certainly do. And she loves me." The smile relaxed a bit as he glanced at Ellie and Billy, who were standing to the side until the examination was completed.

"Are you going to spoil her rotten?" Mama's gaze hardened, wrinkles deepened as she waited for the answer.

"Only if you want me to," Duke said, as his eyes twinkled.

Mama burst into a guffaw and slapped his shoulder. "All right, you'll do. Come on into the house."

In the parlor, Mama poured tea and Ellie passed it around. When everyone had a cup, Mama set the teapot down. "I should tell you, I've been seeing Mr. Johanson up the road after church sometimes. I expect he'll be stopping by one of these days."

"Really?" Billy grinned.

Ellie touched her arm lightly. "Well, good for you, Mama. You deserve some happiness."

"He hasn't said anything serious yet. Only been a couple months." Mama shrugged. "After we visit a bit, I'll take you around the farm so you can see how things are doing. The wheat came in heavy after the rain, but we didn't get much for it."

Duke set his teacup on the saucer. "Sorry to hear that."

"It's the whole country, going through this dry period. I'm grateful that you two did all right this summer," Mama addressed Billy and Ellie.

"Maybe more than all right," Billy said as Ellie took the bundle of bills out of her reticule.

Mama's eyes grew big as she looked at the cash. "I don't think I've ever seen this much money in one place. It looks kinda purdy, don't it?"

Everyone laughed in agreement.

"Let us pray," Mama said and all four heads bowed in unison. "Dear Lord, thank You for the bounty that You led Billy and Ellie to collect in Alaska. It will allow us to keep the farm. And thank You for this new son-in-law who I expect will add a great deal to this family. Amen."

Ellie and Duke exchanged smiles as they echoed, "Amen."

Yes, Ellie thought, Duke would add a great deal to her family and her life. She couldn't wait for their marriage to unfold, one beautiful day at a time.

ABOUT THE AUTHOR

Lynn Lovegreen was lucky enough to grow up in Alaska. Her family was stationed there when she was six, and they fell in love with the place. Alaska's been home ever since. She's always felt the power of words; she taught English for 20 years before retiring to make more time for writing. When not writing, she loves to spend time with family and friends, read, travel, and shoot at targets with her cowboy action shooting club, the Alaska 49ers. Her young adult historical romances are set in the Alaska Gold Rush, a great time for drama, romance, and independent characters who made their own way in the world. See her website at www.lynnlovegreen.com. You can also find her on Facebook and Pinterest.

Thank you for your Prism Book Group purchase! Visit our website to enjoy free reads, great deals, and entertaining, wholesome fiction!

http://www.prismbookgroup.com

Made in the USA
Charleston, SC
22 April 2014